Also by Ray Ordorica

The Alaskan Retreater's Notebook
Caracas Caper
Casablanca Caper
Sixty Years of Testing Guns

BORDER CAPER

by
Ray Ordorica

ISBN: 978-0-578-45547-1

SHEEP CREEK PUBLISHING
NORTH FORK, IDAHO

Special thanks to Richard Weyand, and to his
brother Ken for getting us on the same page.

NOTE: The information given here on the volume of drugs entering the United States is accurate as of the time of writing. The United States is the world's largest consumer of illicit drugs.

TABLE OF CONTENTS

CHAPTER 1
Mole

The old coyote was hungry. He heard them coming as he lay in the soft night air under a yucca bush, his gray muzzle touching the ground. His back and joints ached from age, but his hearing was still excellent, as were his eyes. He smelled them now in the still-warm December night. Patient as time, he watched and waited. The two women spoke softly, but their quiet voices were loud to the animal, who could easily hear a mouse half a foot underground. The women walked by within ten feet of him. As had been his lot all his long life in the desert he had a sense of anticipation that guided his actions. He cautiously followed the two women as they walked across the empty desert, keeping out of their sight and making not a sound.

"*Véngas*, Maria. Come, girl, drag your fat belly over here. It's not far now," Carlita Morales spoke to her cousin in Spanish. The two Mexican girls were both pregnant, and both were walking across the New Mexico desert in the early night air, still almost hot despite it being December. The sage and yucca bushes slowed their progress because they had no light to see the rough trail that their *coyote*, or guide, had pointed out just across the border. Once they were well on the north side of the border the trail became harder to find.

"Carlita, our flashlight is totally gone. Dead. How are we supposed to find our way now, eh?" Maria threw the thing away, adding one more piece of trash to the vast volume of every kind of merchandise tossed by incoming hordes of illegal aliens along every yard of border between Mexico and the United States.

"We can see pretty well by moonlight, Maria, so don't give up. It can't be far now."

The two young girls, just out of their teens, were sure that if their babies were born in the United States the kids would be legal U.S. citizens, and would also have a far better chance of making something of themselves in the U.S. than in drug-torn northern Mexico. Well into their pregnancies, they sold what few possessions they had, gathered all the money they could, and gave most of it to the *coyote* guide to get them safely across the border.

The crossing itself was easy. No border guards, no police of any sort. They were acting, like so many before them, on what amounted to an invitation to cross the border to get guaranteed low- to no-cost hospitalization, offers of jobs, schooling for themselves if they wanted it, and for their children, in Spanish-speaking classrooms.

"Why should we stay home?" Maria asked Carlita before that night's journey. "*Claro que sí*, we'll go north to the Land of Plenty and have our babies in the *Estados Unidos*."

Neither girl was married. Maria was pregnant by her sometimes boyfriend, a drug-runner for one of the Mexican cartels. He was generally never around, but stayed long enough and often enough to take full advantage of the young Mexican girl.

BORDER CAPER

Maria's friend Carlita was not involved with anyone, but when she heard about Maria's plan to have her baby in the U.S. she thought, "Why not have a U.S.-born baby?" She found a willing older man in the form of the *patron* where she worked as a house-cleaner and general *criada*, or maid. The older man, Juan Cordota y Carazco, had had his eye on her for some time. His wife died some years before, and though he was much older than Carlita he was still vigorous and somewhat athletic. One day Carlita gently and carefully approached him. She wanted a baby, and discussed it with the *patron*. Carlita told him she wanted to have the baby in the *Estados Unidos*. Juan Cordota was up to the task, and soon enough Carlita was pregnant like her cousin Maria.

After some months, when the baby was starting to show, Carlita's *patron Don* Juan Cordota made her a gift of all the required cash to leave. He told her, "Carlita, *mi hija*, I have grown fond of you. I want the very best for you and the baby, and this drug-torn country is no place to raise a child. I want you to have your baby in America and if you can find it in your heart, please let me hear from you when the child is born. I promise you I will always be your *patron*, and will provide for you and your child whatever you need. All you have to do is ask."

Juan Cordota was extremely wealthy, as Carlita knew, though she did not know exactly how he came into his money. She believed he inherited it. He never told her anything about his business, and she left it at that.

He told her, "If you ever need anything while you are in the U.S. and cannot contact me, here is the phone number of an associate of mine in the Las Cruces area." He handed her a small business card with a Mexican man's name and phone number on it. "Just tell him you are my niece, and he will help you. Now, *vaya con Dios, amiga.*"

"*Don* Juan, I promise you I will let you know how things are going. When I have the baby his name will be Juan, or if a girl, Juanita. I have grown fond of you too, and it pains me to leave you, but before I have the baby in the *Estados Unidos* I'll need some months to get settled there so the baby can come into a good home. Thank you for your generosity and kindness. I will never forget you."

Carlita sold or gave away most of her things, and with the money from Juan Cordota the necessary financial considerations of the border crossing were made easy for both of the girls.

Maria's boyfriend took both girls to meet with a rough-looking man of indeterminate age at a bar in the small town near where they lived. Ramón Sapresta turned out to be the *coyote* who set up the crossing, led the girls to the border, and sent them on their way. The girls found that out when Maria's boyfriend left them alone with Ramón and went off on business of his own.

The girls each paid Ramón the *coyote* a huge sum to get them to the border and across it. The two girls could have crossed the border themselves, but they had no idea where the best place was to cross, or what to do once they were on U.S. soil.

"*Hijas*, here's some bottled water and a few snacks to keep hunger away on your walk." Ramón handed them the food and water. "You'll be looking for a little shack out in the desert. Look for a blue light. It comes from the window of the shack, and in the dark night you'll see it easily. The man there in the shack is a friend of mine and he'll take you to a good place to sleep, and help you find jobs. That's what you're getting for this money you gave me. My friend there will make sure you get a good start in your new lives in America."

He drove them to within half a mile of the border where old Mexico touches New Mexico, gave them a rough map and a flashlight, and then guided them through the brush and cactus to the crossing point. "Okay, girls, there's the trail. Follow it carefully and stick to the obvious path. That little map I gave you should help you find it. It's not hard."

"What do we do if we get lost?" Maria frowned.

"If you get lost and it gets light out, lie down and rest, and wait until night again. The man will only be at the shack at night. But you won't get lost. The blue light is easy to see from a long way off as you come in from the south. You'll be all right."

Ramón did not tell them that normally the man on the U.S. side would try to make prostitutes out of the girls, unless, of course, they were pregnant — as both these girls were. Ramón said to them, "My friend will get you jobs at one of the fast-food places in and around El Paso. After you get settled you stay in touch with him, eh?"

After they had the babies, well, they owed his friend a favor, didn't they? This supposed debt made it that much easier to make them into hookers. That was the plan if they couldn't find work by themselves. The girls were led to believe they would actually receive something of value for all the money it cost to get across the border, but all they got was the satisfaction of having their kids become genuine U.S. citizens, and that they brought a kilo of cocaine into the country.

Just before the girls crossed the border Ramón Sapresta gave each of them a bag. "Ladies, each of you take one of these bags. Don't lose them! When you get to the shack give the bags to the man there."

Each plastic bag weighed about a pound and was filled with an off-white substance, which Maria guessed correctly was cocaine. She never would have guessed each bag was worth about $15,000.

Ramón continued. "Be sure you deliver the bags to the man at the little cabin. If you show up without the bags you'll be brought back across the border, back here to Mexico, and you'll get a good beating...or worse!"

Carlita spoke up. "You say we won't get lost. How far is it from the border here to the little shack in the desert with the blue light?"

"It's only about two miles, so rest assured there won't be any problem finding the cabin in the dark. Now you better get going. *Buena suerte.*"

The girls stepped across the border and walked off into the night, heading north to their destiny. They had enough light in the late-evening dusk to see their way until they got well across the border, but night comes fast in that part of the world, and it would soon be pitch dark. The girls pressed northward across the quiet desert and were soon out of sight.

When Ramón could no longer see them he crushed out his cigarette, drove to the nearest town and made a phone call. When the connection was made, he spoke two words: "*Dos. Ahora.*" Two. Now.

Across the desert walked the two pregnant girls, sipping on the bottled water they had been given. After the cheap flashlight died a sliver of moonlight provided their only guidance. They could not keep quiet, although the *coyote* guide had told them they had to be silent if they wanted to get to the rendezvous in the dark. "Keep quiet and keep walking, he told them. Follow the obvious trail until you see the blue light of a little hut. In that hut will be the man who will take you in. Don't make a lot of noise or he might put out the light."

But their chatter really didn't make a whole lot of difference. The desert was quiet, they spoke in soft tones, and there were no human beings there to hear them.

The old coyote trailed a hundred yards behind them, following their ceaseless Mexican chatter. The words meant nothing to him, but the sound told him they were nervous and somewhat frightened. He felt his stomach complain as it had done for several days now. He missed a chance at a quail just that day at sundown, and the wasted effort cost him. The hungry animal kept doggedly on the girls' trail.

In a tiny cabin in the New Mexican desert not two miles from the Mexican border and about ten miles west of the extreme outskirts of El Paso, Pedro Gonzales chewed on a cold tortilla. The stillness of the hot night was broken by soft sounds coming from a small portable radio that played jangling pop music alternated with Mexican *ranchero* songs. Pedro sat and waited for the newcomers.

A short, somewhat overweight, swarthy man of forty, Pedro wore old clothes of a khaki color, but they were clean. Yet somehow he managed to make them look dirty, perhaps because of his droopy mouth, wispy moustache, and stringy hair. With that sloppy appearance his clothes couldn't possibly be clean, could they? Or so people said. Life had not been kind to Pedro, but he was not one to complain. He came to America legally when he was twenty-five and had always struggled to find work. He took things as they came, and when this job came to him he welcomed it. He'd been short of cash for a long time and was unable to keep a steady job. It wasn't his fault, he thought, he just didn't like settling down to only one thing.

He'd been a janitor, garage assistant, even a short-order cook for a couple months. One day his streetwise girl cousin, ten years younger than Pedro, came to him with a proposal. "Pedro, you're a patient, trustworthy man," she said. "How'd you like to turn that into a few extra bucks?" And of course he jumped at the chance to sit in the desert for hours waiting for someone to bring him bags of drugs.

Now with this job in the desert picking up the cocaine packages he had time and money to sit and drink some beer with his friends, who always wondered how Pedro was getting along so well. He never told anyone. Pedro was not stupid. He had a small apartment in El Paso, and kept it reasonably clean. It gave him a place to sleep when he was not with some *puta*, one of his whore friends. He usually slept alone.

Pedro had a 'special' phone in his El Paso apartment. It was given him by the people who paid him, and he was not to use it for his personal calls. He had another phone for that. The special one rang only for the higher-born border crossers, not for every *peon* who crossed day and night looking for jobs picking cotton. Pedro was called only for the better-quality incomers. They were the ones who brought in the cocaine. Pedro's special phone rang late that morning.

Maria's boyfriend made the call. "Pedro, there are two girls coming to see you this night in the desert. Be sure to light the blue candles and wait for them, eh, *amigo*?"

"*Bueno*. I'll be there." At sundown Pedro drove his old car west into the desert to the end of a barely marked dirt road, parked, locked the car, and walked a mile to the tiny camouflaged cabin. Once inside, he lit two candles behind a south-facing window that had a blue shower curtain across it, and then settled down to wait. Sometimes he had to wait until the early hours of the morning, but he didn't mind. The pay was extremely high, and all he had to do was keep quiet, and deliver the packages of cocaine the incomers always brought to a lockbox at a storage facility outside El Paso.

He'd take the incomers to an apartment complex and make sure they got rooms. Once the incomers — most often they were women — were installed in one of the apartments, Pedro's job was done. The women, he heard, always got jobs within a day or two and were for the most part quite pleased to be new U.S. citizens. He was supposed to tell another man, a pimp, about any suitable young women coming in across the border, but he never did. "They've got a hard life in front of them without facing that kind of shit," he said to himself. That night he sat in the tiny hut and waited.

Nearly dozing, Pedro jerked to attention when he heard footsteps approaching the cabin, but they came from the wrong direction. Had the new *chicas* got themselves lost? A powerful flashlight cut through the night and Pedro knew this was not the arrival of border-crossing girls. "¡*Chíngame!* Is this a raid?" Where could he hide? He put his hand on the old Walther PPK 380 in his pocket, but before he could get it out there was a soft knock on the door. "Not a raid. Raiders don't knock. It's probably those two bastards again. What do they want this time," he wondered.

He opened the door and saw that it was indeed the two rough-looking *hombres* that had come by his cabin once before. These two *culos* looked like very hard men, thought Pedro. Both had beards, one of them neatly trimmed and the other one shaggy, like Bin Laden's. They kept their hands in plain view, so Pedro withdrew his hand from his pocket and left the Walther where it was. As before, one of the visitors, the extremely ugly one with the shaggy beard that didn't quite hide his damaged face, spoke with a guttural accent, saying in English, "¡*Hola*, Pedro! How are you? You remember us?"

"*Sí*, come in, *amigos*. What can I do for you this night?"

"Pedro, we'd like you to leave," said the other, well-groomed man in excellent Spanish. But not before we have a beer together." He held out a six-pack and an envelope.

The last time Pedro saw them the same thing had happened, but without the beer. They had simply asked Pedro to leave the cabin and not come back for twenty-four hours. Pedro didn't want to leave. "I'm meeting someone," he argued.

The swarthy man then handed Pedro a thick manila envelope, which Pedro opened. Inside he found a huge stack of twenty-dollar bills, which he later counted as $2,000. The well-groomed man said, "The package you're expecting will be here on the table tomorrow."

Pedro then bid the two gentlemen a good evening and walked out into the night. This time the beer was extra, a gift from old friends. Pedro took a beer and the unopened envelope, cracked the beer open, lifted the can to his *compadres*, took a good swig, and walked out into the warm night air.

The two men each opened a can of beer and sat and waited. One of them spoke. "Achmed," said the ugly one, "I am looking forward to this meeting with these two girls. It should be lots of fun."

"I don't think the girls will think it's all that much fun, Osmar. Now be quiet so we don't scare them away." Achmed spoke in clear unaccented English, but with a slight lisp.

Osmar had a particular deformity that made him uglier than he normally was. His face was badly burned in a conflagration with some rebel factions in the Mideast some years before, and he was self-conscious about it. As a result of his disfigurement he always struck out with the ladies. They could not stand to look at his face, and as a result they rejected him. They'd done so all the ten years he carried the disfigurement. This constant rejection left him severely frustrated, and he developed an attitude that if the girls didn't like him they could all go screw themselves. He enjoyed taking his rage and frustration out on the girls in the form of punishment, and that generally meant the whores he was able to pay for, who were able to overlook his ugliness for enough money, didn't live past their first engagement with the man. Osmar had come to enjoy the 'wet work,' and this new job out in the New Mexican desert would let him vent his rage frequently. So he was promised.

The two men silently sat, waiting. The blue light bouncing off the window covering made them look dead. After an hour the soft night sounds outside the little cabin gradually diminished to nothing, and the men knew the girls were near. They both rose.

"There it is!" Carlita spotted the blue light first.

"Finally! It's been half the night!" Maria too saw the blue light in the small window of the desert shack. They made their way slowly to the door and knocked.

The door opened and Achmed, in his excellent Spanish, said, "Please come in ladies. We've been expecting you. Welcome to the United States of America!" He confirmed they were both pregnant, and both about five months along. He said, "Alright, girls, first, have a *cerveza*. Then we have to walk a bit, maybe half a mile, to the car and then we'll take you to your new quarters in El Paso. Can you do that?"

"Yes, of course we can do that," said Carlita. "Let's go! I want to get settled, and begin breathing the good air of the United States." Both young women were excited, and eager to start their new lives in their new country. They'd follow these *hombres* anywhere. They handed over the two white packages of cocaine, which the ugly, surly fellow put into a plastic grocery bag and placed on the table. "Someone will come for that later," Achmed explained to them.

The four of them, each holding a can of beer, walked from the cabin toward the west, not east toward the parked car, but the girls didn't know that. After about half a mile they came to a low area in the desert, where an ancient well had created a sinkhole or depression about thirty yards wide by three yards deep. It provided good shielding from the slight wind. "Well, here we are," said Achmed in his excellent Spanish.

"What's this?" Carlita asked, as she looked around at the sinkhole. "Do we camp here?"

"No, *Señorita*, you die here," said Achmed.

She turned around and looked at Achmed, who seemed to be pointing at her. With a shock she realized he had a gun in his hand, a big ugly gun with a fat tube stuck on the front of it. She started to say something, but then she saw a few sparks of burning powder flare from the gun. She didn't have time to register the dull pop made by the silenced weapon before the bullet smashed into her brain and she knew nothing more. A second later Maria also fell dead, just as she started to scream.

Osmar, with a smirk on his ugly face, went to work with his sharp knife.

The old coyote had lain in the desert scrub fifty yards from the cabin, waiting. He watched the girls knock on the door and enter the cabin. Not long after, he saw them come out with two men, who led them across the desert. He followed, ever more curious. They were heading for the old dry waterhole the coyote knew well. He padded along and watched and waited.

BORDER CAPER

When they reached the sinkhole, he heard a muffled pop, a brief scream and another pop, and then nothing. The pops scared him and made him run off. He took shelter a few hundred yards away under the brush in a shallow hole and waited. He had not long to wait. The coyote heard the sounds of men talking and on the warm breeze smelled a familiar and welcome smell.

The old coyote lay where he was a long time after the men left. The smell lingered, and finally drew him to its source. He made his way slowly upwind, his senses on high alert. He was always careful, had always been careful, and that kept him alive all these years. He smelled what he wanted. He drooled. He knew caution was best, so it took him an hour, circling ever closer, very slowly, looking everywhere, until he was at the source of the smell. He sniffed, gave the equivalent of a coyote's smile, and began to feed. An hour later he was joined by another coyote, and by that time the old one didn't much care who joined him. Dawn approached, and the two animals fed, napped, and fed again.

Billy Vindbraaker flew low over the New Mexican desert south of Las Cruces, not far from El Paso. The previous summer he'd completed his Pietenpol, an experimental home-built airplane which he constructed over a four-year span. His wife died six years ago in a car accident, and Billy received a big chunk of money from his wife's insurance. He was a stock investor, traded online, and was fairly good at it. With some of the insurance money he expanded his online stock-trading business. It went well, and in short order he arrived at the point where his future was assured. He spent only a few hours each week on his computer to make enough money to live fairly well. With no children and with his wife gone, his modest needs helped make that easy.

Grieving from the loss of his wife of nearly twenty years, Billy at first found himself at odds with himself. He brooded and started drinking too much. But luck was with him. Before he turned into a raging drunk he had the good sense to realize what he was doing. He needed a project of some sort to occupy his mind. He decided to build himself an airplane. Others had done it, Billy knew he was good with wood-working tools, so why couldn't he build one himself? He got a set of plans for the Pietenpol Air Camper, an old, simple, and proven design, and went to work.

Soon after he began the task he found the project did indeed take his mind off his sorrow. He got caught up in the project, worked hard and steadily, and made quick progress. Along his airplane-construction trail he managed to get a private pilot's license, flying out of Santa Teresa airport in a Cessna 152, the standard training aircraft known the world over. Despite his hard work it still took him more than four years to build the little airplane. His woodworking skills paid off. He did a really good job on the odd-looking airplane. The wing of the Pietenpol was suspended above the fuselage, attached to it by struts. This wing setup, called a parasol because of the resemblance to a common umbrella, gave the pilot excellent vision below the airplane. The cockpit was open, with just a small windscreen in front, and the struts and antique-looking structure gave the airplane lots of drag. That meant it flew slowly. It was a great airplane for going slow and looking at things on the ground, and Billy did a lot of that. He enjoyed the breeze that got around his windscreen into his goggled face. He'd been flying it now for about six months.

He took off early that morning, while it was still relatively cool in southern New Mexico. On that particular day Billy decided to fly out over the desert down toward the border to see how many illegal aliens he could spot. It would be interesting, he thought, to get some idea of how many were bold enough to cross in mid-day. He considered taking water balloons along to bomb the interlopers, but thought better of it. "No, I'm up for a good time, not to bomb someone or get shot at by a pissed-off drug 'mule' crossing the desert."

He flew low and slow, enjoying everything he saw on the ground. He saw several antelope, one jackrabbit, and one or two coyotes running from the sound of his engine. The breeze from the Corvair engine's propeller made him forget the building heat of the morning, on what promised to be another warm day in the winter desert. The light airplane performed well in the morning air. He flew farther south than ever before, pushing close to the border. His portable GPS unit told him exactly where he was, so there was no problem with his flying too far and accidentally entering Mexican airspace.

It was nearly eight o'clock that morning when Billy spotted the little shack, far from any road, and about two miles from the border itself. He flew close to it and circled, but saw no one. Half a mile to the west he spotted a splash of color in a depression in the desert, and as he flew by it he also saw a pair of coyotes biting and scratching at the cloth, ignoring his engine's noise. He could not make out what the thing was, but it appeared to be two piles of rags with dirty brown stains on them.

He circled to get a better view, flew lower, just 50 feet above the desert, and carefully side-slipped to see exactly what was down there. Just as he came into good range of the two piles of rags, one of the coyotes gave a tug at the cloth and the result was the pile of rags turned over, and Billy was staring into the dead face of a girl with a ragged hole in her belly. Some of her face was ripped away. Much of the flesh on both arms and legs and around the ragged hole was eaten away. That ragged hole was the center of attention of one of the coyotes. Completely ignoring the noisy airplane, he stuck his head into the hole and brought out a bloody chunk of something from inside the girl's belly. Billy Vindbraaker screamed, overdid the rudder controlling the slip and nearly lost control of his airplane. Then he knew he'd have to clean the airplane, because he lost control of his stomach, up came his breakfast, and Billy just missed getting it over the side of the open cockpit.

Sheriff Bytalot of Las Cruces took a helicopter to the site, which Billy had marked with the GPS unit in his airplane. After Billy threw up and was heading back to Santa Teresa airport, he had the foresight to fly back over the two bodies and press a button on the portable GPS unit in the airplane to mark the spot as a waypoint, which meant he could simply give the GPS unit to the helicopter pilot hired by the sheriff's office, and the chopper pilot could fly a beeline to the spot. The sheriff and pilot brought the remains of the two bodies back to Las Cruces.

The news made the local paper, and though the identities of the girls were not yet known and some details were left out, the careful removal of their unborn babies was mentioned.

In a small house down a dirt road out in the desert, thirty miles outside of Las Cruces, a surly looking, Mexican-born man finished reading the report and threw the paper down onto his immaculate floor. *"¡Caca! Otras mujeres pobres. Que lastima. ¡Madre de Dios, venga, amigo!* Come down here, my friend!" Modesto Pincata y Buena, known by his friends as Mole, picked up his telephone and dialed an unlisted number in Idaho.

CHAPTER 2
Rico

It was another of those days Rico Morgan wished would just disappear. The dead gray sky gave a false light to the dawn so you couldn't guess what time it was by looking outside. The leaden heaviness of the cloud cover came down to nearly blanket the ground. The cold fog obscured the surrounding mountains and even hid the far side of the little pond that began fifty yards from Rico's window. The pond was covered with thin ice and a skiff of new snow. Peering out the window of his bedroom Rico could just see the tops of the trees barely lit by the dim light, so he figured it must be late enough to get out of bed.

He rose with a curse. Though in his prime, Ricardo Henry Morgan was already feeling the pains and aches from a lifetime of outdoor living and adventure that left him with scars and bruises, some to his psyche and a whole lot more to his physical body. He donned an old robe and dragged himself to the kitchen, let his dog Birdie out to see what was new down by the partially frozen pond, then heated up a cup of yesterday's coffee. Rico always made coffee the previous evening so, as he always told anyone who asked, he wouldn't have to wrestle with it first thing in the morning and screw it all up whilst in a sleepy fog. He'd been there and done that enough times to have learned better.

As he drank a cup of his beloved organic dark Sumatra and pondered his day, Rico Morgan's thoughts turned to Las Vegas and the upcoming Shooting Hunting and Outdoor Trade Show. "Can I find a way to attend SHOT? Probably not. Do I even want to go?" Rico thought. He used to like going to the show to see all the new guns, and to see how many of his old shooting-buddies-turned-gun-writers showed up. He'd bump into 'em in the crowd and try to remember their names, and when he last laid eyes on 'em. Occasionally he ran into Diane, the woman he used to love. The last time he saw her was six or seven SHOT Shows ago in Dallas. "Heck, I've moved on," Rico said to himself. "And what would Sally think about Diane?"

Sally, his current lady, didn't know about Diane. Rico didn't know exactly how he felt about Diane after so many years, but he thought about her from time to time. Would it have worked out? Rico doubted it. "But it maybe would have been worth the effort to try." Rico was thinking himself into a dull funk over his morning coffee.

"Why bother going to SHOT at all?" he thought. "Three or four days of that show grinds me into the ground. It's all old hat. Even the new stuff is old, 'new' exciting calibers that were first brought out a hundred years ago in England or Germany. Nuts! Maybe by now they're all digital," he chuckled. "Or they're laser guns like from Star Wars. Hell, everything else is digital these days. The new John Rigby outfit might come up with a double rising-bite 470 with digitally controlled firing pins and a laser sight, but somehow I doubt it." Rico chuckled again. "Good on Rigby for getting back to England where he belongs," he said to himself.

"But such is life. You get what you can along the way, and the Devil take the hindmost." Year by year Rico's thoughts of Diane became more and more vague and foggily remembered. Could it be his age? Nah, he wasn't getting old, just getting better. Something like that.

In the middle of Rico's brown study the phone rang. Rico was old-fashioned enough to despise Caller ID. He also hated microwave ovens and cell phones. He never carried one of the pocket jinglers unless it was necessary in the course of his work. He picked up the land-line phone with a hearty "Hello?"

"¡Hola, amigo! ¿Qué pasa?" was the response. It was Rico's Mexican friend Modesto Pincata Buena, whom Rico had known for many years, and whom Rico trusted as he trusted no one else.

The two friends exchanged a few pleasantries, and then Modesto asked, "But Rico, how come you are still sitting there in Idaho, my friend?"

"I live here, Mole, or did you forget?" Rico called him by his nickname, which he thought was the only appropriate name for a fellow who spent so much time at his small ranch in the desert that Rico called a hole in the ground.

"*Claro que sí, amigo,* but why aren't you down in New Mexico with those *federale* friends of yours looking for the loony who cut up some more young women? Or isn't that in your line of work anymore? It has been so long since we worked together, maybe you forgot what it is you do for *dinero,* eh, *hombre*?"

"Hell, why aren't you out there yourself seeking revenge, since it's right in your backyard? Or don't you do any of that stuff anymore yourself?"

"Hey, man, you really should read the paper or watch TV once in a while so you know what's going on in the world," said Modesto. "Or even better, turn on Alex Jones or Rush Limbaugh. Anyway, the cops think these gals were probably hauling some drugs over the border, cocaine or heroin or something. The girls were pregnant, and maybe they had the stuff tied under their bellies or stuffed you-know-where or something. They got hit about forty miles southwest of Las Cruces, out in the desert, not far this side of the border. Some guy flying out of Santa Teresa spotted 'em and called the cops. Rico, this is something I believe you need to look into. Seriously."

"Well, I haven't heard a thing about it. Fill me in. Cut up how? How many girls?"

"Two girls were found in the desert, not far from the border. Their clothes and a few personal things found by the cops indicated they were from Mexico. They were murdered, shot in the head, and then their babies were cut out of them. No trace of the babies remained in the area. Thing is, another girl was found about a month ago, her baby cut out of her, and her body dumped in the desert off that little haul road going northeast outa Las Cruces. You remember that road?"

"Sure," said Rico Morgan, "that's the way to the old White Sands Missile Range, or to the Organs if you keep on going. There's not much out there."

"Right," replied Modesto. "There've been rumors of some others, too, but these two new ones, they were coming in under the radar, got helped across the border, but no one knows where they were going or what they were gonna do when they got there. Probably just coming over to have their kids become U.S. citizens. Only thing anyone knows for sure is they're dead, and their babies are gone. Hell, nobody would've ever found the bodies if that local pilot hadn't seen 'em from the air. Nasty shit. The kind of thing I thought you might know somethin' about."

"Good God no! That's sick stuff. I recall some poor babe washed up near Chicago a while back. Knifed, cut open, and dumped in the lake. But how do they know dope's involved?"

"Well, they don't, but most of these crossing people bring in something before they disappear into the dust of the border states and start getting free everything from us taxpayers. The cops guessed they'd have some trace of drugs, checked, and found it on the clothes. The drugs got everyone's attention, but some cops, a few smart ones, don't think dope was the main reason for the hit. The stuff these border crossers bring in is just extra payment for the guys who take 'em in and get 'em jobs, or a place to stay, or a hooking gig with a pimp. The real question is, Why did they take the unborn kids? Even more important, what're you going to do about it?"

Rico pondered this a while, staring out the window at the dead gray sky. A pair of Canada geese flew over the pond and circled, thinking about settling in to the small bit of still-open water. Rico's dog Birdie kept her eyes on the geese and smiled at them. The pair changed their mind, apparently not liking the presence of the golden-haired dog just a touch too close to the pond for comfort.

"Hey Rico, you still there?" asked Modesto.

"Yeah, Mole, I'm here. Just got to thinking about Las Cruces and the old times, and about little Ricki whom I maybe should've married, and about you and me and those hot Chevies and our races across the desert to see who could get to Juarez first with the fewest speeding tickets. I'm remembering all that good food in Old Mesilla, the whole space-exploration crew we worked with, fresh seafood in the middle of the desert at Tegmeyer's Steakhouse, and all kinda good ol' stuff. Now, why'd anybody want to cut up a couple of girls in that beautiful hot bitch of a desert down there. Know what I mean?"

"So how soon you get down here, Rico?"

"I'll contact Boise Control and meet you in El Paso in two days."

Two days later a tall, slender, athletic-looking man, sandy haired with touches of gray, blue eyed, resembling a skinny version of Chuck Norris without the beard with a little James Coburn thrown in, and dressed as though for golf, got off the late-afternoon Delta flight at El Paso airport. A black-haired, shaggy-looking Mexican with a small beard, wearing a battered broad-brimmed hat and with the remnants of an ancient multicolored blanket slung over his shoulders like Clint Eastwood wore in the great 'spaghetti westerns,' met him with a brief handshake.

"Rico, *amigo*, good to see you." Modesto Pincata Buena had ancient eyes with crinkles at the corners. He looked a lot like the Mexican actor Arath de la Torre, with an even more piercing gaze. Though only a little older than Rico, Modesto's early life had been hard, largely due to the poverty of his youth and growing up in dark and nasty corners of Mexico City. He was about as street-wise as anyone could get, having put in his younger years in that enormous city, but he managed to avoid the gangs and the crime rampant in old Mexico. It had not been easy, and he had the scars to prove it. Modesto Pincata Buena crossed the border legally in his late teens, landed in Las Cruces, and worked hard at whatever he could find to do. An uncle of his died and left some money for Modesto to go to college, so for a few years he attended the University of

Michigan at Ann Arbor, where he met Rico. When the money ran out he went back to Las Cruces.

After a year or two Modesto got a job at the White Sands test facility, where he once again encountered Rico, and this time they got to know each other really well. Rico was working on a temporary job on a space-flight project, a different task from what Mole did. Rico moved to Las Cruces for a couple years, though still maintaining his home base in the Denver area where he then lived. The two hit it off and became fast friends. On completion of the space-flight project Rico and Modesto and their girlfriends went camping together in the high country of the Colorado Rockies. A year later the two men hunted together in Montana, then in Africa, and a few years later all four of them went to Australia.

As time and money permitted, the shared adventures of the men continued, and their trust and respect for each other grew stronger over the years. When Rico set up his current business of private high-end investigations it was natural for him to include Modesto in his plans They had worked together on several dangerous missions, and this was looking like it could be another one.

The Mexican man knew Rico would most likely get involved eventually in the ongoing butchery of the pregnant women, but phoned his Idaho friend to speed up the process. Now they were back on the hunt together in Texas, hunting the most dangerous game.

The two men walked in silence to the baggage area where Rico picked up his small black Samsonite suitcase and walked out into the warm desert sun. They got into an old, battered-looking, pale-green Chevrolet Impala. Mole drove north, picking up the main highway out of El Paso toward Las Cruces.

"*Oyes, Pinche Buey,*" said Rico, gently fouling Modesto Pincata Buena's name. "How come you're still drivin' this beat-up junker? Bet it's got two hundred thousand miles on it by now."

"More like two hundred fifty, *Pobre,*" retorted the Mexican, calling Rico by his opposite name, poor instead of rich. Mole spoke perfect English slang. His voice sounded like someone who had lived in Detroit all his life, not Mexico City, but he often lapsed into Mexican street lingo like some bum who could barely speak English. "But the engine's a hotted-up 350 now, fuel injection, turbocharger, the runnin' gear's all brand new, and she'll do better'n a hundred and fifty. Tires are Eagles, she's got the latest ABS brakes, stiff suspension, roll bar, best shocks, new transmission and rear end, all stuff straight offa Daytona. The only thing old is the looks."

"Spiffy!" said Rico. "Neat!" He well knew the value of a hot car that didn't look hot. "Hope we don't need all that power this trip."

"You never know," said the Mole. "So why Las Cruces?" He asked.

"Boise Control suggested we start with the sheriff there. Control seems to think he has some info that could bear on this situation. We'll see what he says and then head back to the border. Maybe drive out, or rent a plane and fly out to where the guy found these dead girls and give it a look. By the way, Control was about to call me when I rang them. Good funds from the U.S. Government, Immigration Enforcement, believe it or not. Good call on your part, *amigo.* And of course they want it kept quiet."

Modesto said, "Border crossings, drugs, dead babes and missing babies. It sounded like big money to me, so I called you. In fact it sounds a whole lot like government in general."

BORDER CAPER

"Yep!"

The old hot-rodded Chevy motored north toward Las Cruces.

Rico Morgan was an exclusive private investigator. His clients tended to be countries or governments rather than individuals. The things he investigated were largely outrageous crimes, high-profile or high-dollar items or situations that had sufficient reward money to pay Rico's expenses and finders' fees to his small 'provider' group in Boise, Idaho, and of course ample compensation to Mole whenever they partnered on a deal. One recent task was the recovery of a collection of extremely valuable coins for a private collector, a job that ultimately took Rico to Alaska and into the bowels of an ancient John Deere tractor. [*The Green & Yellow Caper*.] Mole had not been in on that one.

Rico's provider group in Boise, loosely called 'Boise Control,' consisted of two men and three women, all found and hired by Rico. The team's leader — though not so designated — was I. Yeats Prunzalot, age forty-three, a highly skilled computer hacker formerly with Assange. His father was Sukkan Dondem Prunzalot, a genius professor of math at Yale, age seventy-four, expatriate from India, who often helped his son with Rico's sometimes strange requests. Rico had taken calculus at the University of Michigan in the same class that Yeats attended, the instructor being another Indian math genius, Rammad Upcha Bhutt. Bhutt had had old man Prunzalot for his tutor. Rico made the acquaintance of Yeats at university, and later met his renowned father on a junket to Europe. Both father and son were about as good at math as Rico was at shooting, but despite Rico's close association with these math genii it didn't help him blaze any trails in the field of mathematics. It was not his thing. Some can see in terms of math like others see in terms of music or painting or photography, but not Rico Morgan. He had the greatest respect for Yeats and trusted his abilities to the utmost, which is why he recruited him when he set up Boise Control. Yeats inherited his father's intellect, and then on his own, as a result of computer-programming classes in which he excelled, turned his abilities and knowledge of mathematics into being able to delve into Internet back doors like the many so-called hackers so prominent on today's TV shows, except Yeats was the real thing.

The second man in Boise Control was George William 'Willie' Kers, better known as G. Willie Kers, age sixty-two. Willie was a retired Chrysler executive who had traveled the world on business and knew people in all corners of the globe. His circle of friends, many of great influence worldwide, was huge, particularly in the far East, including China and Taiwan as well as in Australia and New Zealand. Willie introduced Rico to the world of late-1980s and early 1990s Chrysler products, some of the hottest production cars ever made in the United States. Willie had promised to find Rico one of the 140-mph four-door Spirit R/T's but instead came up with a Dodge Stealth R/T twin-turbo V6 with six-speed gearbox that was even faster. Rico was quite fond of G. Willie Kers, and greatly valued his world-wide connections.

Myrtle Stockwood was a former call girl, now married and in her sixties. She knew people as few people know people. She had a way of gathering insight that most would not catch. A flicker of the eye, a slip of the tongue, a slight shift of one's attention spoke volumes to Myrtle. Many times her insight into the human psyche had been of invaluable help to the team and to Rico.

BORDER CAPER

The newest member of Boise Control was twenty-three-year-old Kikkan DaKrotch, a brilliant Dutch-born college grad who majored in Political Science. Her lengthy treatise on world politics had earned her a nomination for a Nobel prize. She caught Rico's attention when she was being interviewed by Alex Jones, shortly after her political essay made national news. Rico asked Myrtle Stockwood about Kikkan, and on Myrtle's say-so instantly put Kikkan on the team.

The final team member was Eileen Tudarite, age thirty-four, who was a former Wall Street trader who got rich, got smart, and got out. She traded in farming futures among other things. Her knowledge of ongoing weather modification made it easy for her to watch patterns in the jet stream, forecast crop futures, and make things happy for her and her banker. When it became obvious changing administrations were altering the way things were being done as to weather modification, Eileen decided she had enough of Wall Street and became a realtor. Rico heard about her success story, interviewed her, and chose her for the team for her great insight into world finance. Eileen was good friends with Donald Trump.

Boise Control found the high-paying jobs by scouring the news, Internet, radio stations, rumors, hidden stories, suspicions, street talk, conspiracy theories and the like, for leads to important unsolved crimes. Anywhere from zero to three times a year they would come up with a set of proposals for Rico to examine. When he chose a particular crime to look into, Control did much of the research and made contacts to verify the funding and give Rico a head start about whom to contact for details. But Rico did all the grunt work, talked to all the contacts, and took all the risks. He did all the traveling and lost all the sleep. He was the one who got shot at.

The group took into consideration Rico's, and often Mole's, special abilities and contacts as much as they were able, based on information Rico gave them and what they could find out for themselves along the way. Another important task for Control was to make sure the jobs had sufficient monetary value in the form of rewards, or percentages of recovered funds and the like, to make it worthwhile for Rico to justify the expenditure of his time and not a little money, and to take the necessary risks. The five people who made up Boise Control all had other forms of income. They did the job-searching only as a part-time venture. This commonly gave Rico plenty of time off, which suited him. Boise Control contacted the organizations, heads of state in foreign countries, or other personnel who were the hardest hit by the various crimes. Control essentially found the money, found the contacts, set up the links, and turned Rico Morgan loose.

Half a mile behind Modesto's hot old Chevy was a dirty black Camaro. The car was one of the old low-slung muscle cars that every teenager had to have, a few years back, so he could impress his girlfriend and his buddies. Mostly he succeeded in impressing the hell out of his insurance agent, who got rich writing coverage for it. This car was long past its prime, now bent and rusty and dusty, but it still had lots of power. It was driven by a Mideastern man with a short, neat, black beard. He was definitely out of his teens. He appeared to be an Arab, but spoke perfect English to his companion.

"This might be our only chance, Osmar. The two ought to be out of the city in about ten minutes, and then you can practice your shooting, eh?"

His passenger answered in thick, guttural tones. "Yes, Achmed, as soon as they get out into the desert I will show them what this is for." He patted the AK-47 by his leg, its stock folded forward for easier movement in the car. "Aiieee, that was some fun with those women! I look forward to the next meeting in the desert."

The other man said nothing. They drove on in silence, stalking the two men in the ancient green Impala.

Rico and Modesto well knew each other's thoughts. They had spent lots of time together in conditions that demanded instant communication and they'd become good at it. Hardly a word was needed when they were both tuned in to a situation. They operated together in the Mideast, and were in Ethiopia as advisers. They hunted Cape buffalo together in Tanzania, fished for shark in Australia, flew over much of Alaska, and camped together with their ladies in the high country of Montana, Colorado, and Idaho. Modesto's wife was killed a decade before in gang-related shooting, and he had not remarried. Rico was engaged twice, but never married. He currently had a girlfriend who was a world-class violinist.

"How's Sally?" asked the Mexican, referring to Sally Foarth, Rico's violinist friend.

"She's doing well, but her touring drives me nuts. We don't see a lot of each other because of it, but it's okay. She's in DC now doing some prep for a two-week concert tour around England. She leaves in a week or so."

They had little need for small talk, and drove on in silence. That silence was broken by Rico Morgan.

"Mole, ol' buddy, what do you have stashed in this heap to take care of varmints."

"You mean coyotes, amigo? I got a Ruger 220 Swift under the back seat," said Modesto Pincata Buena.

"I mean two-legged coyotes, my friend. We've got a couple back there a ways that seem to have glued themselves to your tailpipe."

"Those guys in the Camaro? They've been there since the airport. I thought you'd seen 'em. There's a 40-cal Hi-Power with Robar mods under the seat in the box. There's a 12-gauge pump, in with the Ruger under the back seat, that Robbie's guys worked over. You remember how to open the box? Where's your piece, anyway?"

"Yeah, I remember. The box opens if you push up, left and back, then pull down. If you had any brains left you'd remember I helped you install it." Rico got the 40 S&W-chambered Hi-Power from the hidey-hole under his seat. The magazine was full of Federal Hydra-Shoks. Rico shucked one into the chamber. "My CCO is stashed in my suitcase in chunks," said Rico. "You just can't Bee-Ess your way past airport security these days. You packin' iron?"

"Do I got pants on? Sure, man, I got a piece. What the hell you theenk?" said the Mole.

"Sorry."

"I figure those *muchachos*'ll let us know what they're up to about the time we get a few miles outa town. There's just about no traffic on this road, so they can stay back, follow us, mebbe try to run us off the road, or worse. How about we pull a brake trick?"

"That's the ticket, if they come up on us."

"What d'ya figure they're up to, Rico?"

"Like the guy with the whip."

"Like what?"

"Like, this guy has a whip hanging on the wall. His buddy asks him what the dickens the whip is all about. The guy says, `It belongs to my wife.' So the other guy asks him, `What does your wife do with the whip?' The first guy shrugs his shoulders and says, `Beats me!' "

"Jeez! If I gotta put up with that crap, I'll let you out here and those guys can have your ass!"

The two men drove farther out of town, taking the highway north toward Las Cruces. The sun slowly sank toward the western horizon. Soon the desert darkness would come, and come quickly.

The dusty old Camaro held back, still on their tail. The driver, Achmed, was thinking of Gerta. Gerta, the lovely German wench had been his contact with the big guys in Washington on his last visit there. She had come in from Germany a week before, met Achmed in DC, and together they met with some politicians there — his paymasters actually. Then he and Gerta spent the night together.

The following day Achmed flew to El Paso and rejoined his partner Osmar, They had a job to do. Gerta told him to watch the airport arrivals from Missoula on this day for a man who looked a little like Chuck Norris, but was taller and skinnier and didn't have the phony beard stubble. "No, he won't be wearing Norris' "Walker" cowboy hat," she said. "He'll be dressed casually. Here's a recent photo of him."

Rico had in fact worn a dark Harris-tweed sports coat over a dark-green corduroy shirt, black trousers and sturdy black shoes.

When Gerta gave Achmed the assignment, she spoke in her native German. "Morgan walks with a springy step, but he's older than he looks and acts. He'll meet a Mexican man at El Paso airport. Get rid of both of them, but be damned careful! You must not call attention to yourself when you do this."

RAY ORDORICA

Achmed easily identified Rico at the airport from the photo, and set out with Osmar in the ancient Camaro to follow and eliminate the duo.

As he drove, Achmed recalled his night with Gerta in DC. They made love brutally, quickly, and coldly. Achmed remembered Gerta's nipples, how they pointed at him like gun barrels, and how she squealed when he bit them just a little too hard. His foot pressed on the accelerator harder, closing the gap between the Camaro and the ancient Impala.

"Don't get too close!" The passenger named Osmar broke into Achmed's thoughts. "Are you all right,?"

"Yes. Just getting a bit excited about, ah, taking them out when we get farther out of the city."

Osmar looked hard at the driver, staring at him as he spoke. "It will be soon, now. Wait until there is no other traffic, then pass them. Get into the left lane and then go by them as fast as you can. I'll shoot the driver first and then go for the passenger. In two quick bursts, the job will be done!"

"No, shoot the passenger first," said Achmed. "If you shoot the driver first the car might swerve into us, or off the road, and you won't be sure of the second shot."

"Good," said Osmar. "Of course I knew that, I was just wondering if you were so distracted by your recollections of that German bitch that you forgot about killing these bastards."

"That, Osmar, would not do, would it?" Spoke the driver with clipped tones.

"No!" came the terse reply.

Darkness came fast and traffic died to nothing on the four-lane highway heading north out of El Paso. The two old cars were alone on the road.

"And now, we attack!" Achmed mashed the accelerator to the floor.

BORDER CAPER

The Camaro closed quickly on the Impala motoring serenely into the desert twilight, and Achmed moved the old car into the passing lane. Osmar opened the window and brought the folded-stock AK-47 up from the floor and held it just below the level of the window, not wanting to give his play away to the two men in the Impala.

"Don't look now, but here they come, buddy." Mole warned Rico Morgan of the fast-approaching Camaro.

"Okay, Mole, let's do it."

The Impala swerved slightly into the left lane, toward the Camaro. The move made Achmed lift off the gas slightly, exactly the effect that Mole planned for. No longer accelerating hard, ready to hit the brakes, the Camaro lost the advantage. Mole in the Impala cut back to the right and slammed on the brakes. The Camaro tried to follow suit but couldn't slow quickly enough, and the two cars came abreast of each other. Rico saw Osmar raise the AK-47 and poke it out the window.

The Arab pressed the trigger in desperation, loosing a burst of unaimed, fully auto fire in the general direction of the Impala, but the bouncing AK was clumsy with its stock folded, and the unexpected hard braking threw the Arab off balance. The shaking rattle of the world's most popular assault rifle was not conducive to quick recovery, and all the shots went wild.

Rico had anticipated the violent braking of the car and had braced himself against it. He leaned over almost on top of Mole's back and presented the .40-caliber Hi-Power out the window as the Camaro came into range. Rico double-tapped the Browning at the passenger, two shots, fast. He scored one hit in the man's upper chest and one dead center on the forehead. The AK's harsh chatter ceased immediately as the dead man slumped. Rico shifted to the driver but the man had recovered his surprise enough to take evasive action, and he braked even harder and swung the Camaro wildly across the highway behind the Impala. Rico didn't get another shot.

The Camaro veered off the road to the right, the east side of the highway, dug into the sandy soil next to the road, lurched, then flipped into the air and turned over, coming down on its roof in the brush at the edge of the highway. It skidded along until it caught on something and flipped over again back onto its wheels. Its engine drove it off the right side of the highway, down a bank and out into the desert.

Mole tried to swing the Impala around to the right to follow, but a steel bridge barrier said no dice. He slowed, spun the car around, raced back down the highway a hundred yards and pulled off the road to the east. The two men looked for the Camaro.

"Watch it, Mole, that guy's sure as hell armed, too."

"Where the hell'd he go?"

"Right down here," said Rico. "I saw him drop off this side of the road right here where the shoulder's gouged. Now, where'd that bugger go? There's some tracks!"

The Camaro had, against all odds, been drivable in spite of its double roll-over, and Achmed had been wearing his seat belt. When the car righted itself he sped off in the direction it was pointing, straight into the desert. The tire tracks made almost no marks on the hard desert dirt. Nothing, not even faint tracks, showed the passage of the car after it got twenty yards off the highway except for some slightly damaged yucca bushes. The fading light didn't help. Rico and Modesto drove back and forth looking for any sign of the car, but found nothing. The winter brush was still springy and bounced back, giving no indication of the car's passage.

"Shit, compadre, how could we lose a whole Chevy?"

"Like that guy with the whip, Rico," said Mole.

"Double shit."

"Rico, the sun's behind us. We'd be sitting ducks if we went out in the desert on foot looking for that guy. I say we call it quits.

"I agree, but man, I sure don't like it. We've got some bozo out there tried to kill us. Let's get on down the road, buddy."

"Maybe we can hide somewhere they can't find us, until we figure this all out."

"¡*Claro!*" Rico agreed.

Mole once again headed the ancient hot-rodded Impala up the road north toward Old Mesilla and Las Cruces.

Out in the desert in a dry wash not a quarter mile from the highway sat the Camaro. The wash concealed the car from the road, a stroke of luck for Achmed. He lay a short distance away, concealed behind some rocks and yucca bushes, clutching a 9mm CZ semiauto and sweating profusely despite the quickly cooling desert winter evening air. As he watched the car driven by the two men swing tentatively back and forth near the road he realized they could not see his car. After a short while he watched them drive away to the north. He muttered to himself as he sat there, the sweat running freely down his face. "Osmar, how could you be so damned stupid as to get yourself killed. And how could I be so stupid as to fall for their crap-trap? My friend, I helped you get killed, and for that I will avenge you. This I promise on my father's grave."

He sat there for awhile after the other car drive off, then stuck the 9mm back into its holster, got to his feet and walked back to the Camaro. He pulled his dead companion out of the car, stripped the dead man's pockets and clothes of all identification, and left the body for the coyotes. He got in the battered car, picked up a portable short-wave radio and spoke curtly into it in Spanish. Then he drove carefully back to the highway and turned south toward El Paso.

CHAPTER 3
Roxy

"**W**ell, amigo, that was interesting," said Rico as they continued north toward Las Cruces in the dimming light of the warm winter afternoon. "What the heck d'ya think that was all about? Are we so famous our showing up in El Paso together caused a panic with some bad guys? I mean, why us? Why now? Any ideas?"

Mole replied, "*Amigo*, maybe they heard you were coming by tapping one of our phones. Or someone told them we were gonna look into these murders and that someone didn't want any interference. But it was pretty fast work, I'd say, no matter how it happened."

Rico and Modesto had a small reputation as independent "researchers" into things like murder, extortion, drug smuggling and other clandestine and illegal operations. They had helped solve enough cases that their small reputation for success was growing in a few law-enforcement circles. The men realized that the two butchered Mexican woman, and reports of other similar mutilations, indicated something extremely fishy, and also quite large was going on. The fact that action had been taken against them so early in the game told them the perps were deadly serious, and the stakes were most likely high.

"Fast, yes, but kinda clumsy. And didja get a look at those guys? They were not Mexicans. They looked like Arabs, or some kind of Middle-Easterners. Who could've told 'em? I didn't talk to anyone but you and Control, so maybe they did tap the phone."

Mole replied, "No, I didn't see their faces very well. I got a good glance at the driver and might recognize him, but the other one I didn't see at all, even though he was closer. I was too busy trying to duck and drive to look at 'em. But...now what the devil is that?" Mole slowed the car. "More trouble?"

"What the hell...!?" Rico couldn't believe his eyes either. There on the side of the road was a car on fire. In the glow from the car, that had apparently run off the road and burst into flames, was an attractive, young-looking blonde girl holding a small day-pack in front of her chest, frantically beckoning for the car to stop. She was wearing neither shirt nor bra. She wore faded blue cutoffs, and her long, slim legs ended in hiking boots. She wore a gold chain around her neck, no other jewelry, and no makeup. Her long blonde hair hung in gentle waves past her shoulders but was not long enough to serve as a cover for her nakedness, so the day-pack had to do. Highway traffic was non-existent, and it looked to Rico like this woman needed help. She was using the pack to hide her upper body as well as she could, and not doing too good a job of it. She clearly was agitated. In the fading light of the desert she appeared to be slightly sunburned, though her skin was dark enough that it just made her look better. As Mole's car slowed, the fire from the hood of the other car went out.

"Pull over, Mole," Rico said. The car pulled to a stop and the girl, bashful now, ran up blushing, the pack pressed to her chest, and said, "Please I need a ride...."

"Yeah, and a shirt, too," said Rico. "What happened?"

"My car suddenly started smoking," she said, "so I pulled over and opened the hood, and a ball of flame came out and set my shirt on fire so I pulled it off. It burned up, and I don't have a spare."

Rico thought she looked a little like Emma Roberts, but better, and with longer, lighter-colored hair. She had the same saucy twist to her mouth. "I'll see if I can find you a shirt," he said. "Mole, pop the trunk please. " He got out of the car and got his small suitcase out of the trunk and opened it on the ground. Both men were trying hard not to stare at the girl. Rico fished his spare shirt out of his suitcase and turned to hand it to the girl only to find she had put her pack on the ground. He barely noticed the Centennial Airweight pointing at his midsection.

"Gee, miss, those are nice...er, I mean, that's a nice gun you have there. What is it you want of me?"

"I just want your shirt, dammit, and no crap from either of you guys." She appeared not quite scared, but maybe desperate. Rico saw it, but he also saw the professional way the girl was handling the gun...finger off the trigger, Weaver stance, gun pointed in the general direction of his testicles.

"Miss, whoever you are, why-ever you lost your shirt, I don't care. If you need help we're not the bad guys. We're here on business and thought you needed help, so we stopped." As he spoke Rico carefully measured the distance to the girl, and snuck a half-step closer. Mole, watching all this in the right-side mirror, saw the play and listened as carefully as he could to the conversation. Still inside the car, he already had his pistol in his hand.

Rico, now barely within range of the girl, turned his head away from the girl and stared hard at Mole, caught his eye, and nodded once. Mole hit the horn and Rico jumped. The girl never batted an eye, simply stepped back quickly in lockstep with Rico, snapped up the gun to cover the center of Rico's chest, and dropped her finger to the trigger. She shouted, "Hold it!"

Rico was fast, yet he was amazed at her speed and her perception of what was going on. He was fast enough to stop himself before the girl began her trigger squeeze, and she was fast enough to avoid killing him. The gun never wavered. The girl was obviously well trained in its use.

"Try any more of that bullshit and I'll take your head off, Bozo," she said. "Out of the car, driver, hands up, and get back here! Do it now!" she commanded, backing away from the two men and keeping the gun exactly between them in the ready position, her eye focused on its front sight.

"Mole, this one's for real! Put your popgun away and get your butt out here and don't do anything else. If she meant us harm we'd both be dead now, partner."

"Okay, Rico, I'm comin' nice and slow," said the Mole.

"Turn around, both of you," she commanded. The two men did as she asked, and she managed to get into Rico's shirt while keeping the men in front of her gun. "Okay," she said, "turn around again." The girl moved back to give the two men room. "Who the hell are you?" She asked.

"I'm Rico Morgan and this is my friend Modesto," Rico said.

"Oh sure, and I'm the queen of Spain out for a walk."

"Miss, I don't know who you are or what you want, and frankly I don't give a damn. If you know my name I wonder why, and why you don't think I am who I say."

She said, "I know very well who Rico Morgan is, and you're not him. I just met him in El Paso and he's younger, and better looking, too. Let me see your identification. Carefully!"

Well, that sure threw a wrench into things, thought Rico. Why can't I be who I say I am? Rico carefully and slowly withdrew his wallet and passed his driver's license and CCW permit over to the girl. "Did you ask to see the other guy's identification?" Rico asked.

She looked at the two licenses with their photo ID's and saw that Rico was indeed telling the truth. "No, because I had agency information, and a photo of him, before I got here," was her reply. "Gentlemen, it would appear I have been lied to by someone. I don't like it, and you can drop your hands now. Here's my ID." She tossed Rico a small leather folder containing her photo. In it was the logo of the CIA, and the information said she was Roxy Roades, twenty-seven years old. Rico could see her photo was a match to her face.

Rico tossed the ID folder to Modesto. "Amigo, I told you she's the real thing. Miss Roades, I'm glad you were well trained, or I'd have eaten your bullet. Why all this bullshit about no shirt?"

She said, "I had info on the car you'd be driving, was told you were an imposter, and I was supposed to stop your car if it came along and hold you guys here. You were supposed to have been stopped on the highway before you got this far, and I'm just the backup. There's a tracker on your car and I've got a portable unit that told me you were coming. I rigged a fake fire in my car, and played the damsel in distress. But my shirt really did get burned, dammit."

"I don't get it," said Modesto. Why stop our car? And you said it was going to be stopped on the highway, but two guys tried to shoot us, not stop us. And who is this other 'Rico'? "

"What!?" The girl was clearly amazed. "I was told you'd be stopped by operatives of another agency. If you somehow got past 'em I was supposed to detain you here and contact my station. There was nothing about any shooting...."

"**GET DOWN!**" shouted Rico, as he dove for the cover of the car.

The shuddering noise of the approaching helicopter was broken by the faster stutter of a machine gun, being fired from the open door of the helicopter, a Jet Ranger. It had come in fast and low out of the sun's remaining rays in the darkening sky, and the gunner had fired just a shade too soon. His bullets tore up the sand and brush where the trio had just been standing. The girl fired two shots toward the 'copter and got up and ran for the other side of the car, which was better cover for the turning helicopter. Rico was right behind her, but Mole was diving for the still-open trunk of his car.

Mole pulled hard and up came the rear floor of the trunk, and from a custom recess Mole pulled out a short, compact rifle with a gray stock and a scope mounted on the front end of its action. It was a Steyr Scout rifle in 308, a handy rifle the late Jeff Cooper made famous. Mole worked the slick bolt and almost casually shot the machine gunner in the helicopter as it bore down on them, just as the gunner was about to fire a second burst. The gunner slumped, and the Jet Ranger's pilot zoomed up and away, picking up speed rapidly. The helicopter quickly disappeared toward the west.

"Nice shot, amigo, " said Rico. "I bet he's going out there to dump the body because there's just a whole lot of nuthin' out to the west."

Roxy noted, "there's a couple of my bullet holes in that bird, so we might maybe get a trace on it."

Rico said, "I guess that's why you were supposed to, uh, *detain* us. Give those guys time to get here if we made it this far and you didn't cap us, and eliminate whoever was left standing. Let's get to town before anyone else tries to take us out. "

Modesto Pincata Buena floored the old Chevy and at a hundred and forty miles an hour covered the remaining miles to Las Cruces in short order.

The two men got rooms at a motel and Roxy went off into the night to try and get some of her own questions answered. She promised to check with them in the morning and let them know what she found out.

———————————————

"We're gonna have a look at the crime scene, where the girls were cut up," said Rico to Roxy when they met in the morning. Mole was off on the telephone to his housekeeper, letting her know the situation. "We'll fly over it and have a look. There's a chance we can learn something. What are you gonna do?"

"I talked with my DC office and they said to fly back there. I'll do that, but there's something they're not telling me. I know I've been screwed with, and someone's gonna pay for it. I'll lie low and snoop around and let you know if I come up with anything."

Rico gave her a number at the Boise Control offices where she could leave a message, and also his home phone number and secure email address. After she finished her coffee she rose and walked out just as Mole was returning to the breakfast table at the little diner next to the motel.

"*Pues*, Rico, you gonna get in her pants?"

"Jesus, Mole, gimme a break. Yes, her trousers look just delightful and entirely tasty, but who knows what she wants. I'm just the butt-headed target out here in the desert, not a stud for every babe who comes along. For all I know she's good friends with Sally. Sally sure as hell spends a lot of time in DC."

"I bet you get in her pants before the month's out. Let's go see the sheriff. "

The two men went first to the Las Cruces office of Sheriff Bytalot and told him their tale. The sheriff knew of them slightly by their reputation and was cooperative, especially when Rico showed him his letter of authorization from U.S. Immigration, but the sheriff could shed no light on the road attack, nor on the helicopter assault. "I just don't know who might be behind all this crap," said the sheriff. "I'd guess someone doesn't want you pokin' inna this double-murder deal. It might be a real good idea to check your six, boys and girls, or just go home and leave the shopping to us."

Sheriff Bytalot told them the approximate location of the attack on the two girls. He had not wanted outsider civilians or any more media hacks poking into the crime scene, but made an exception for Rico. Rico told him he wanted to fly over the site to get some photos that he'd share with the sheriff, which Bytalot cheered. He told Rico to fly a compass heading of 195 degrees southwest from Doña Ana airport and he'd get to the crime scene, still marked off with police tape, about two miles north of the border with Mexico. Rico suggested the sheriff might want to take a look both to the east and to the west of the highway about eighteen miles south of Las Cruces to see if he could find a couple of dead bodies.

BORDER CAPER

At the Las Cruces airport Rico rented an older Cessna 172 from the FBO, got a check ride with the local instructor, and then piled Mole with Rico's good camera in the passenger's seat and took off again with full tanks. They flew southeast, following the GPS of Rico's iPad Air2 equipped with WingX flight map to Doña Ana airport and then turned southwest, following the sheriff's rather vague directions. Rico watched the iPad's air map carefully to avoid Mexican airspace.

"Jeez, Mole, there's nothing out here at all," said Rico into the intercom mike. "Sage and more sage, with a lotta sand in between. This close to El Paso you'd think there'd be some signs of life. Those tracks or trails could be from bikers or critters. Mebbe the townies come out here on dirt bikes. You see anything?"

"Yes! Off to the right below the nose, I see some colors that don't belong."

"Let's have a look, eh?"

Rico pulled back on the throttle and pulled a notch of flaps to get the speed of the 172 down, and turned a big circle that brought him over what turned out to be the crime scene. The yellow police tape was still there at the sinkhole. He flew east half a mile to the shack, and circled hard to the left so he could see the area. The shack was maybe ten feet on a side. He banked steeply to the right and circled again so Mole could get a good look and some photos.

Mole said, "How about we get closer to the border and see if we can pick up some sort of a regular trail. It looks like there's a vague path from the shack heading south. It's over there now." Mole pointed to the left.

"Got it!" said Rico, as he headed the bird along the vague path. They were not far from the Mexican border, augering toward it at 90 knots. When they got within half a mile of the border Mole saw a deep arroyo strewn with the colorful junk so many border jumpers tossed away, useless garbage carried that far as a last tie to the home country.

"There's a junkyard in a gulley over on my side. You got anything over there?"

"Mole, I see a whole lot of sand over here. Let's get a little closer south."

In a few more spins of the propeller they got as close to the border as Rico dared go. He turned the Cessna to the east, toward El Paso.

"Mole, I'm gonna put the sun at our backs and fly back west along the border a way, see what's what."

In about three minutes he circled back and put the border just outside his left window. Mole kept his eyes on the Border-Patrol road that followed the border a short distance to the north. Rico looked for a crossing. "Rico, I see the shack, way over to the right."

"There it is! I found the crossing point over on my side. There's a low spot in the desert and right in the middle of that the sand doesn't look right. Looks like it's been brushed over to hide footprints. The brushed area's not big, but comes right to the fence, and it looks like the path north begins right there."

"It does. There's the path," said Mole, looking out the right side of the airplane. "It's heading north to that dumping ground."

"So that's the crossing," said Rico. "And nothing but drug country to the south."

Later, on the ground at the airport, Rico scratched his head thoughtfully. "So, what do we know now that we didn't know yesterday? The murdered girls were probably crossing the border along the trail we saw. We already knew that. They were killed half a mile from the shack, so the perps knew about that sinkhole. I don't think we need to go there."

"No, *amigo*, the cops would have looked it over pretty well. The sheriff said he didn't find anything there that led to anyone in particular. But how did the keeper of the shack know the girls were pregnant? Does he always cut up pregnant girls?"

"No. There must be dozens of pregnant women come through there, and most of them make it to El Paso."

Rico considered this as they got in the car and headed back to the highway. "The sheriff said he knew of some half-dozen girls who had babies in El Paso after crossing. They must've been carrying when they crossed. And if the guy at the shack was killing them regularly, word would get back to Mexico and this place would be shut down. That means...."

"Someone else comes to the shack and takes care of the women, but only if they're alone, not too many of 'em at a time, and no men with them," Mole continued. "How does he take care of the normal shack guy, or guys? Probably one guy. There can't be a whole lot of people involved in these border crossings. What if...."

"Someone pays him off to leave the shack. That way he can come back to the normal routine, but gets cash to duck out when certain pregnant women, maybe at some predetermined stage of pregnancy — and alone, like you said — are coming across. That means someone in Mexico must be telling the killer or killers these targets are on the way."

"I think that's it, my friend. Most likely a border guide, or *coyote*, would know what to look for in the women going across, and he could phone someone in El Paso and let 'em know that, say, two lone pregnant women are coming in a day or so, maybe even the same day, and the bad guys go to the shack, pay off the compadre there, and wait for the girls. The girls would not know the bad guys from the good guys, so they'd go quietly to the sinkhole."

The two friends drove back to their motel.

Over a late dinner Rico shook his head and said, "Mole, what say we take a few days off. I gotta get back home and take care of winter business at the ranch, and I need to clear my head about all this stuff."

"Yeah, so do I. I'll get you to El Paso tomorrow and you can be home by nightfall."

Back in his motel room Rico phoned in a flight reservation for the next day and hit the hay.

CHAPTER 4
Home Attack

Rico and Modesto returned to their respective homes, Mole to his little ranch out in the desert outside Las Cruces, and Rico to his digs in Idaho. The two men needed to get caught up on personal projects, never mind the convolutions of deep mysteries at the Mexican border. For Rico that meant bringing home his three critters from the loving care of his female vet friend Andy, plowing snow, hauling and cutting up dead trees for firewood and, especially, getting a clearer mind to do some deep thinking about the whole state of affairs.

Roxy Roades, the CIA agent, phoned Rico soon after he arrived home. "Rico, I've got nothing so far. Wanted to try out your phone number, and see if you had anything new to add."

"We didn't learn much from our fly-over at the border, Rox. We found the beaten path to the shack, but I'd bet a shiny nickel the crossing place is gonna change, with all the official attention being brought to the old place."

"I bet you're right. You catch anything on a Jet Ranger with holes in its hull?"

"*Nada*. Nothin'. No Jet Rangers for rent for 500 miles. That one might have come in from Mexico, for all we know."

"Okay, Rico. So, watch out for low-flying choppers. I'll be in touch."

Rico and Modesto had essentially drawn a huge blank on their trip to the border, and Rico didn't like that.

Mole also phoned Rico. "*Amigo*, the dead girls were autopsied and they were clean of drugs. Nothin' bad inside their systems. So it looks like they were just coming into the country to have their kids so they'd be U.S. citizens. They brought whatever drugs they carried as part of their crossing deal."

"Hmmm. I wonder if the murders are drug related, though, buddy. Yes, I know the drug volume coming in from Mexico is really bad. Massive, actually. Maybe we need to find out more about it. I know a little, but I bet our buddy Eduardo in Mexico knows a whole lot more'n I do."

"Hell yes! He deals with it all the time, one way or another."

Rico replied, "Still, I just can't see this murder business being tied to drugs. I've gotta think about it some more before we dig any deeper. I'll talk with you in a couple days. Watch your ass. We're both targets."

————————

Rico Morgan wanted a cigar.

Like Sherlock Holmes, Rico always thought better under the slight and pleasant influence of a bit of nicotine, and he needed to do some really serious thinking. Someone was trying to kill him and his buddy and presumably anyone else who was in close contact with him. Like Roxy.

He went to his tobacco cache and rummaged around among the bundles of stogies stored there, all kept at sixty-five-percent humidity and sixty-five degrees. The cigar selection called for serious consideration. The stogie had to be big enough to last a while, so that meant none of the Habanitos or Cubanitos that were tasty, but too small. And it ought not to be an all-day sucker like those huge Gurkha and Hoyo de Monterrey Churchills that went on and on. Not a Cuban. Rico had only a couple of the contraband smokes left anyway, and they were for extremely important events. Maybe a Fuente Hemingway Signature...naw, too big. Rico settled for a Hoyo de Monterrey Maduro Robusto, clipped the end of the short, fat cigar with his vee cutter, toasted the other end, walked outside and lit up.

He always smoked outdoors. Neither he nor his dog nor the two cats liked the stench of dead cigar smoke. The late-winter Idaho mountain weather was mild that day, so a light coat, his old green Eddie Bauer down jacket with most of the down long gone, was all he needed. Rico went for a short walk down to the stream leading into the little pond on his property, and as always, along came his dog Birdie. She always walked in front of him and told him what was ahead. That let Rico lose himself in his thoughts of the past few days. After a short walk through a few inches of late-winter snow (a welcome change from the previous winter's four solid feet of white feces, he thought), he arrived at his favorite Ponderosa overlooking the stream, cleared a spot on the ground at the base of the old tree, and sat down to think. He carried a small insulated pad to sit on so he could smoke and think in comfort without rushing things or freezing his ass.

"Now I can dig into this, Birdie, and try to make some sense out of it." He stroked the golden dog's head between her upright ears as she sat quietly near him, puffed on his stogie, and started the gears going in his head.

"Money comes easily to the gangs that rule the borders," Rico thought, "so with that kind of ready cash available why would they go after pregnant girls? And not every pregnant girl at that. Only those who were about five months along, and maybe not all of those either...not so far as we know. Not enough data. Were the girls being cut up solely for the babies? Did that make any sense? Were there more drugs hidden inside them, special types of drugs that wouldn't show up in autopsies? Was someone using the unborn babies for some sort of satanic ritual? And if so, why so many?"

There didn't really seem to be any good use for dead babies, or if there was, Rico could not see it. A few weeks past he'd read about some ghouls selling parts of them, but the really big money was just not there, nor was it worth the risk to take these babies out of dead women and rob the drug lords at the same time. Nothing seemed to add up. What if they left the drugs? That was a possibility. That meant the drug lords were unconcerned.

"Why does someone want me dead? Am I too close to something I'm not supposed to find out? Do I know something incriminating I don't realize I know? What could it be?" He stroked the golden dog's head and puffed on his stogie.

"We've been to southern New Mexico. We saw the border country of the desert there and even the bleedin' murder scene. We saw the path coming from the border leading up to the little shack, and we looked into the sinkhole where the girls died. From the air it looked like an eye. . .the eye of death." Rico remembered nearly every word he and Mole had with the Las Cruces sheriff about the tragedy. "And we got exactly nothing for our trouble. There has been precisely no light shed on any of these mysteries. . .except that Roxy was set up, most likely by her own CIA."

So far as Rico could tell he didn't know anything more than he knew before he'd left Idaho. All he gained from the trip was a bird's-eye look at the crime scene, which gave him a vague idea how the murders were done. When Mole phoned him and told him to come south Mole hadn't told Rico anything that wasn't in the local New Mexican newspaper. "Well, Birdie, could it be the bad guys are wrong? Could it be they think I know something I just don't know? If that's the case, what in hell is it they think I know?" Rico was getting a headache.

His thoughts drifted back to the last time he saw his girlfriend. As a gifted classical-violin soloist Sally Foarth played all over the world, traveling frequently. She owned a small home in east Idaho not far from Rico's digs. The last time he was with her 'out on the town' she played a concert in Missoula, in western Montana. The event was small but formal, and despite Missoula being pretty much an 'overgrown cowtown' in the eyes of some of Sally's fans visiting from LA, the gathering was also attended by at least two senators, one of them the supposedly gay old coot Larry Likkaman from Idaho. The congressmen had been in the area at the time, so it was said. Rico remembered he approached the two politicians at the reception after the event. He came up behind them with Sally on his arm, and vaguely recalled the two quickly changed the subject of what had been an animated discussion. The two congressmen glared at Rico until they noticed he had the star of the evening's performance on his arm, at which point they both became politicians again, which is to say they were all smiles and bullshit.

Rico had seen that change of face many times before, the typical double face of your professional liar, or politician, whatever you wanted to call 'em. Yet something Rico thought he heard one senator say had stuck in his memory. It had sounded like, "We simply have to get more, and the Mexicans are a good source." Another man had muttered something about too many potties, and where to put 'em.

Rico thought the discussion was about an impending road-improvement project in western Montana. It had been much discussed in the local news and in Idaho as well. The discussions centered on the unlikely fact the road project would make first-time use of a novel design of Mexican-made, low-priced, modular portable toilet never before imported into the U.S. In addition, there was talk of importing Mexican workers for the job as part of the deal. The importation idea came out of DC and was in the trial stages of voter acceptance. Not many people in western Montana were out of work looking for jobs, so once the project began there would be a huge need for outside help. As might be expected, the project was not popular in western Montana, nor anywhere else, for that matter.

"These DC bums are here to push that lousy deal," thought Rico. "Why else would these high-priced hucksters be here? It's a heluva long way from DC to Missoula." Even though he thought the worst of them, he forced himself to returned their false smiles, tit for tat.

Sally introduced Rico. "Senator Likkaman and Senator Grafter, this is Rico Morgan. Rico, Senators Larry Likkaman and Hugh Grafter. Larry's from Idaho."

They shook hands, and the Idaho senator's limp handclasp confirmed to Rico what he had heard about the man. Still, he felt compelled to make at least a slight effort at cordial conversation.

"Senator, I couldn't help overhearing you talking with Senator Grafter about getting more workers up from Mexico and about these new Mexican potties. I know the Mexican-made portable johns are a fraction of the cost of those made here, but are you concerned there will be too many and you won't know where to put 'em? And I'll bet you a dollar there will be plenty of Mexican workers on the road-construction team whether or not you bring in any men along with those modular toilets.

The senator had coughed hard, then turned slightly pale at the question, but then he composed himself and gave a feeble grin. "Yes, we, ah, wondered where to put them because there are so, ah, so many. I guess we'll let the man in charge decide where to hide, er, where to locate the, uh, *potties*." Both men then excused themselves. Rico noticed Likkaman a short time later leaving the reception with a younger, slim, and somewhat oriental-looking man. Likkaman's choice of companion for the evening again tended to confirm Rico's suspicions that the dear senator was gay.

That night in bed he asked Sally about the senator's tendencies. Sally spent lots of time in Washington, DC, in concerts and on PR-planning trips for international music events, and she knew many of the bigwigs there.

"Yes, Rico, he's a confirmed fag but he denies it. Bad for the image, and worse for his re-election chances, I guess, if he outs himself."

"Didn't seem to hurt Barney Frank," said Rico. Isn't it a coming trend to admit to homosexuality whether or not you are, or approve? I mean if the guy admits he's a committed fruit it might actually get him more votes come the next election. It sure would in California, but of course he's from Idaho, and there aren't a whole lot of cowboys coming out of the closet here. 'Ride 'im cowboy' still means a horse, not some other guy's butt."

Sally said, "I know. Guys like you would probably shoot 'em."

"Nonsense. Just because I don't approve doesn't mean I'd like to shoot 'em. Not all of 'em anyway. Maybe only every other one. I mean, with all the good things that can happen between a man and a woman, why would anyone want to change that?"

After a pause, Sally asked, "Did you want to *talk* about sex, or...?"

It had been a good, if tiring, night for both of them. Rico recalled their night together vividly with a slight smile as he sat in the cold with his dog and his cigar. He spoke to his dog. "Birdie, I wish Sally were not quite so popular. I'd like to see her here more often. She could give up all that traveling, give up Bach, and play bluegrass fiddle to my banjo pickin', and we'd have a grand ol' time. Or I could learn to play the fiddle and go along with her. Play duets around the world." He sucked on his stogie a while. "Fat chance, eh *amiga*? You think I'd have a rough time of it?"

The dog smiled at him with her soulful eyes. "*Ruff!*" She agreed.

Later in the day Rico phoned his Mexican friend and reported no news, but added, "*Amigo*, I suspect someone thinks I know something I don't really know. But I can't figure out what it might be. And you're in danger because the bad guys know if I knew something serious. I'd have told you."

"*Claro que sí*, Rico. Certainly. But you can't think of anytheeng it might be?"

"Nothin', my friend. Not a bleedin' thing. Only thing sticks out is maybe one dumb night with Sally and some politicians, but that don't make a lick of sense to me. Talking about some porta-potties."

"Well, then, call me when you have maybe thought of sometheeng important, okay? I have a hot date with a *señorita* this evening, and you nearly interrupted my plans."

"Sorry about that, ol' boy. *Adios*." Rico slowly hung up the phone.

There had been a slight click in the line as Rico and Modesto broke their connection. Rico had waited for it, and heard it after Mole hung up. He put down the receiver with a thoughtful expression.

"He's there, but it don't sound like he knows shit about anything secret, like that guy tol' us he did. I think we oughta drop this gig, take our money and run." Jake Auffe, a rough, dirty, heavy-set man in his late forties was dressed like a local rancher in a beat-up poncho, work shirt, old jeans and run-down western boots. He spoke to another, younger, man who looked like he was just out of high school. The younger man, Dick Gabler, had long greasy hair and wore a gray sweater under his old winter coat. He wore jeans and battered hiking boots. They'd listened to Rico's phone conversation with Modesto while sitting in Jake's old beat-up car several miles down the road from Rico's home. The phones in the area all were serviced by outdoor boxes, or posts, out by the road where the underground optical cables came up for each ranch or house and became hard wires, which made phone tapping easy if you were disguised as a phone serviceman. The phone post near Rico's small ranch had been rigged with a small transmitter tap, and his phone conversations were relayed via high-frequency radio to the listeners a few miles away.

Dick Gabler spoke. "I don't care if he knows shit, and I don't care if he can quote Einstein in Greek. We've got this job to off this guy because he knows too much about somethin', and we gotta do it so we can collect the rest of our dough. At least we know he's home. So let's go get the sumbitch."

"Let's wait at least until dark, another hour. Even later'd be better. Let him doze off first."

"Man, it's too fuckin' cold in this part of the world. Let's head south once this is done, okay?"

"Shaddup. Quit your complainin', Dick. Jes' count your money."

"I ain't got no fuckin' money yet, Jake. Not until this is done. But then I'll have ten grand and a ticket to Hawaii. Fuck this shittin' cold!"

Jake pulled out a 45 auto and skillfully checked to see that there was a round in the chamber. Dick Gabler did the same with his 9mm, but only because the older man had done it, and Dick thought it looked cool. Dick was young and eager, but stupid. The job for which the pair had been hired seemed to demand of Dick that he look tough and competent, even though he was neither. He didn't know a lot about guns, but he felt compelled to put on a good game face, and play the part of the tough guy.

As Dick tried to press-check the gun for a chambered round, the gun slipped and he nearly touched off a round in the general direction of Jake's leg.

"Watch what you're doing, fool." Jake had seen the young man fumble

"Screw you, Jake."

Dick scared some girl at a bar the previous night by claiming he was a "perfessional assassin," as he put it, and he and Jake had to leave the bar quickly because the frightened girl called the cops and they were on their way. Dick never killed anyone, but Jake had killed two men, one while he was in the service and another in a fight over some whore in Memphis when the other guy pulled a knife. Jake shot him but got off on a self-defense plea. Jake and Dick met at a bar in Salmon, and both shot their mouths off while drunk. A dark-complexioned man overheard them at the bar and hired them to do this job.

They were supposed to listen to the tapped line, make sure the man was home, and then go blow him away. When Jake asked why, the man told him, "Because he knows too much." The dark man said they would be paid ten grand apiece for the job. He gave them a thousand dollars each before the job. Jake and Dick were skeptical until the dark man showed them the rest of the money, so the pair agreed to do the job. The dark man who hired this doubtful pair was quite certain they could do a job as simple as walking up to the door and shooting whoever answered it. He had not counted on Rico Morgan's careful reactions to possible threats to his life.

Rico figured his phone must have been tapped sometime before he left for El Paso. Either that or Mole's phone was bugged. One way or another the El Paso hit men knew he was on the way, and laid an ambush. The fact that Roxy was there too meant serious long fingers into the depths of the CIA, and that meant deep-cover involvement, which translated into serious trouble for Rico from dedicated hit men.

Rico looked into his phone line as soon as he returned home. He checked the line junction at the street with a bug scanner, found the bug, left it in place, went home and thought about it. He figured whoever wanted him dead would try for him again one way or another, and would most likely use the tap to find out when he arrived home. As soon as Rico used the phone for the first time on arriving home, which he just did to call Mole, he alerted whoever was listening. Rico figured he could expect deadly company in the near future.

After he hung up, Rico went into immediate action. He secured Birdie in one of the back rooms of his house and armed himself with a modified M14S semiautomatic 308 rifle equipped with a night-vision optic hung on the business end of its 2-8X Burris scope. He dressed in his arctic overalls and boots, warm hat and gloves, and slipped out of the house at full dark by one of its not-so-obvious exits.

He carefully moved to the thick brush that lay beneath the apple tree some twenty-five yards from his front door, and concealed himself behind a low rock wall. A light coating of snow reflected the dim moonlight oozing through the overcast sky and gave a ghostly look to the landscape. He had an unrestricted field of fire toward his front door.

The M14S was a trusted weapon put together on one of the excellent forged Chinese Polytech actions by Clint McKee, top dog at Fulton Armory. It featured a Winchester barrel, all G.I. parts, walnut M14 stock, vented forend, and Rico's home-made custom flash hider. It used to have a Leupold Mark 4 ten-power sniper scope on it in a Brookfield mount, but after trying it Rico thought it was too much scope for close-range work. The 2-8X Burris made a lot more sense. The rifle's trigger pull had three-point-five pounds of take-up on the first stage, and a one-pound pull past that, dead clean. The ammo was 168-grain Federal Gold Medal Match.

The night-vision device on the front of the scope had an infra-red beam that permitted unlimited vision in pitch-black darkness out to nearly a hundred yards. Rico had the night vision turned on to pierce the shadows of the murky night. The house was in total darkness. Anyone seeing it would think everyone inside had gone to bed. He waited patiently.

It was nearing midnight. Rico, cold and miserable despite his heavy clothing, was about to give up and move to Plan B, which was going inside, having a shot of cognac, going to sleep in his warm bed, and doing the same thing the next night. Then they came.

A car drove past slowly, heading north. The two amateur hit men drove past the entrance to Rico's small ranch, turned around and came back from the north, passed his driveway again, then slowed and parked the darkened car a hundred yards south of his driveway. Rico heard two car doors close, which meant at least two shooters. He heard muffled voices. This told him these were not pros, but still a deadly threat if they came to his house. They came. He watched the two men walk into his driveway and proceed the seventy yards up to Rico's front door in absolute silence, handguns in hand.

Rico peered through the night-vision device and examined their faces. He had never seen them before. One of them stepped to the side, to be able to direct fire into the open door more easily. Rico did not have a pushbutton bell on the door, so the pair were forced to knock. They rapped on the storm door, then opened it and beat on the inner door. From back in the depths of the house came the sound of Birdie barking at the intruders. Rico was tempted, but knew he couldn't just pick 'em off. That'd be murder. After a few minutes they knocked again and he decided to challenge the now fidgeting pair.

"What do you want?" He called.

Young inexperienced Dick Gabler, nearly beside himself with nervousness, heard the challenge and spun toward the darkness behind him. Although he could see nothing but an apple tree, its bare branches reaching for the sky in the darkness, he raised his pistol and took hasty aim.

"No! You fool, don't shoot!" shouted Jake. But he was too late.

Dick cut loose with his many-shot 9mm into the darkness in the general direction of the apple tree. Jake started to run, but Dick's luck ran out. A full-patch 308 bullet caught him in the center of his chest, penetrated his heart, passed completely though him and lodged in the huge old Ponderosa next to the door.

Jake ran like the wind, slipping here and there on the snow, but managing to keep his feet. Rico did not shoot again. Jake got to the highway and fled to his car, and Rico heard him drive away to the south as fast as he could go. "I guess that bozo can take a message to his handlers," said Rico to the night air.

He phoned the sheriff, and in a few hours the remains of Dick Gabler were removed. Rico told his friend the sheriff he got a good look at the remaining man but did not recognize him. Shortly before dawn Rico finally went to bed.

The second gunman, Jake, rocketing along the highway in his old car, finally slowed to the legal limit. There was no traffic on the dark, winding, two-lane highway that late at night, no lights in his mirror. Jake knew he wasn't being followed. It didn't pay to go flying off the road. Sweating hard from his mad run down Rico Morgan's long driveway and a hundred yards more down the highway to the car, Jake finally caught his breath. "Dick, you stupid shit, you coulda got us both killed." Jake said it out loud. "I'm gonna keep the money that bastard paid us. The risk was part of the payment whether we got the job done or not, so that guy can go whistle if he wants a refund. In fact I'm gonna ask him for the whole fuckin' thing. No goddamn guarantees in this bidness," he cursed. Half an hour later Jake was home.

BORDER CAPER

Late the next afternoon near sunset Jake drove to the lonely little bar where he had met the dark-complexioned man who paid him and Dick to do the job on Rico. The dark man was there, sitting and waiting at one of the little tables. Jake sat down and ordered a beer. Only after it came and Jake had swallowed half the beer did he allow himself to look at the other man.

The dark man had been patient. "Well?" he asked.

Jake looked around the nearly empty barroom and leaned forward over the small table. "Nix," he said. "The guy knew we were comin' and set a trap for us. My loudmouthed asshole buddy started shootin' at the frickin' moon when some noise spooked him. I tried to stop him but the stupid shit let fly and got hisself shot. I took off. What were we supposed to do?"

"Ah," said the dark man. "He found the phone tap. Did he see you?"

"Obviously he found the tap, and he must've seen me, cuz he was outside watching us knock on his friggin' door. But it was pretty dark, so mebbe he didn't get a good look at me. So what do we do now?" Jake swigged his beer.

"We do nothing. You're done."

"What about the rest of my pay?"

"You didn't finish the job. I should ask for a refund." The dark man got up, clearly disgusted, and left Jake sitting with his hand wrapped around his nearly empty beer glass. Jake called for another beer and watched the man leave.

The dark man, whose name was Robert "Bugs" LeProsy, walked out, made sure Jake was not following, cut down a side street, and went into a convenience store. He made a cell-phone call to Senator Larry Likkaman in Washington, DC. With his caller ID the senator knew who was on the line, so he answered the same way LeProsy had spoken to Jake.

"Well?"

"Our local heroes failed. One is gone. The other was most likely seen and might be identified." Bugs LeProsy lit a cigarette.

"Fix that," said Likkaman and hung up.

Back at the bar Jake, now finishing his third beer, was getting hungry. It was full dark out now, and long past Jake's dinner time. He decided to go home for dinner and grab something out of his fridge. Jake didn't like cooking, so since Janet left him he'd subsisted on quick dinners, not cheap but fast. He had a freezer full of them, and that sounded better to him than another box of Chinese take-out shrimp-fried rice. Janet took the dog when she left, there were no kids, so Jake didn't have to deal with anyone but himself.

He paid his tab, made his slightly tipsy way to his car parked just around the corner of the bar in a dark side street, and got in. Fumbling for the key slot, Jake was suddenly aware someone was in the back seat. He turned to look at the intruder and opened his mouth to say something, but never got out a word. Two silent bullets penetrated his forehead and made a jumbled mess of his brain. Jake slumped sideways onto the seat, letting out a gentle sigh as he collapsed.

After a substantial wait Bugs LeProsy got out of the car and walked away.

———————

The next morning Rico removed the phone tap from the connection box. He didn't tell the sheriff about the tap. The local sheriff knew Rico's reputation, but Rico didn't want him to know he was being targeted. If he knew, the sheriff might take some protective action Rico didn't want, which would generally complicate things. However, to prevent any further dangers to himself and his dog and whoever might visit him,

BORDER CAPER

Rico decided to sleep in one of his outbuildings. It had a wood stove and a rough bed, and some electronic warning measures. Rico's best early warning system was Birdie. Her keen eyes, ears and senses always surprised Rico with things she could see, smell, hear, even feel, far beyond his poor human abilities.

At sundown Rico locked his two cats in the main house and he and Birdie settled into the rough shack. Rico quickly got a decent wood fire going in the small stove and cooked a simple dinner on top of the firebox. He fed his best friend and gave her one of her favorite treats, a dried pig's ear. He settled back on the bed with a short glass of Speyburn on ice and shared his thoughts with Birdie.

"My friend, why are these bozos trying to kill us? What did we do wrong?"

Birdie was concentrating on her treat at the other end of the bed and did not answer him.

"I mean, things are getting downright dangerous, my dear dog."

Birdie growled softly at a difficult bit of ear. Rico heard a hearty crunch, but no words of comfort.

Rico sat and thought for a long time, long after Birdie fell asleep on her insulated rug on the floor. Finally Rico fell asleep too, but it was an uneasy sleep.

That night around four a.m. a soft *whuff* and low growl from Birdie got Rico fully awake instantly. Gun in hand, he slowly cracked open the oiled and silent shutter covering the small window in the shed and peered out. A young raccoon was grinning up at him. The 'coon smelled the remains of Rico's simple dinner and snuffled around the little shack looking for a handout. The animal was one of Rico's wild friends. Rico spoke to him gently, put out some dry cat food for the masked rascal, and went back to bed.

The next morning Rico's mind was made up. It was no time to sit around and wait, he thought. He secured his beloved dog in the house, got in his car and drove to a nearby restaurant to use the phone. No phone tap there! He called Mole in New Mexico. Rico had emailed Mole about the attack the previous day.

"Mole, let's take the battle to them instead of waiting around for them to come to us. I have an idea where to start."

"*Pues, amigo*, it's about time. I got some visitor the other day too. Some fool tried to put a knife in me, but he slipped, and ended up sticking himself. So where are we gonna go, and what are we gonna do when we get there?"

"Mole, we need to find out who's sending these killers to our doorsteps. We've gotta check and make sure we're on the right track. What say we go visit Eduardo in your home country and see what he says about drugs crossing the border. Maybe he can give us some clues about what we're not seeing."

"*¡Claro que sí!*"

CHAPTER 5
DC

In a small, undecorated, white-painted room at the end of a long corridor in a building just off Capitol Hill in Washington, DC, three men were talking heatedly in low tones.

"We need more time," said Senator Larry Likkaman, the pseudo-conservative from Idaho. He wore a shabby dark-gray suit that looked about as tired as his worn face.

"But we need more product, and we need it now!" The Chinese envoy Wun Thik Dik responded in near-perfect English. In his late 30s, he was slim and trim in a tailored Hong-Kong best-quality black suit and appeared to be extremely fit. A slight hint of mint wafted off of his body into the dead air of the little room. "We have an agreement, a deal as you say, and you are not keeping up your end of it."

"But Mr. Wun, one of your goons got killed last week by that meddling bastard, so we're short a man. The other fellow can't do any, er, business until his partner's replaced." This from Senator Hugh Grafter, the aging Democrat from New England. "And that won't be easy." Grafter's triple chins blended smoothly into a cream-colored shirt covered by his newish brown three-piece suit.

"He was not my 'goon,' as you call him, but one hired by your country, paid by your country's money, and therefore one of *your* goons," said the slim Chinese man. "And we did not expect your team of goons to suddenly become general assassins, sent on a road trip to eliminate a potential threat that proved to be too much for their humble skills. Or should I say, half the goons died because of their incompetence! But despite that, we will see if we can come up with a prospective replacement."

"Another Arab?" asked Likkaman, with evident disgust.

"Would you prefer a Jew? We could probably find a suitable Mossad man, if you prefer," said Wun Thik Dik with contempt equal to the senator's disgust.

"Just get us someone. We could get someone from our own branch of government, but we don't want to tap any sources outside our immediate control, and most certainly not Mossad." Likkaman picked up his old BlackBerry from the table and prepared to leave. "I still think we ought to have more teams."

"No!" Grafter and Wun spoke in unison. "There is too much risk, and there would be too much exposure too soon," said Grafter. "We have the devil of a time with disposal as it is. And you want two or three times as many? That would shut us down instantly. What about that meddling pair of bums from Montana?" Grafter continued. "Is it so hard to get rid of them that it has not yet been done?"

"We are working on that as we speak," said Likkaman. "And they are not from Montana. One is from my backyard, in Idaho."

Wun replied, "The other is, I believe, a Mexican national. I don't know why you don't simply deport him. Or would that be 'politically incorrect,' considering your open-border policy to the south?"

"He's not a Mexican. He's an American citizen," Likkaman assured him. We looked into that already."

"You can find out his citizenship but cannot tell us his whereabouts or his movements? Isn't that wonderful, " said Wun. "At least we know the Idaho man has a girlfriend, and therefore a built-in weakness, one we can exploit. And who knows what *she* knows by this time."

"Do what you need to," spoke Likkaman. Just get rid of both of those men. We don't need them looking at this any further. They have a reputation for getting results, the kind we don't need in this affair. We don't know what they uncovered in New Mexico, and we don't really know how much they overheard at that concert in Montana. Was he putting us on about the toilets? Is he really that thick?"

"He is anything but thick," said Wun. "The remaining team member assured me of that, and also, his reputation is well known. We should have kept our mouths shut at that concert instead of talking about how to dispose of dead bodies. And then that clown asks us about potties! Does he think we're that stupid?"

Grafter cut in. "The Mexican toilets were indeed in the news, and that might really be what he was referencing."

Wun continued. "Horse manure. At any rate, we are quite certain the cowboy didn't learn anything new in New Mexico. Really, there was nothing to be learned. He left almost immediately, and there has been no action taken by him other than responding to both our attacks on the highway. There is nothing to tie us to the, er, *potties*."

With a resigned sigh, Likkaman spoke. "All right, we can do no more at this time. I'm taking heat from my authorizing a

CIA agent to act against him. I had to lie to quite a few people that I had valid information, had to act quickly and, well I guess you know how the game is played. So it's settled. We need another man. You, Wun, will provide him, and we will clean up the loose ends. We'll meet here again in two weeks."

The three men left the room separately, a few minutes apart.

In another room in that same building a slender young woman with long, light-brown wavy hair took off her earphones, and carefully removed the memory card from a recorder that had captured the entire conversation of the three men. She put the card into a hidden compartment inside her purse and locked the recorder into a desk drawer. She rose to leave and caught her reflection in a wall mirror near the desk. She tossed her hair out of her face and smiled at herself. Her long hair hung to the level of her breasts, which pushed firmly against her white blouse. Her maroon skirt stopped above her knees, and she wore black, modestly high-heeled boots with rounded toes. She hated the current trend in women's fashion for 'butt-stickers,' which she called the pointed-toe boots so many women favored. A thick black belt circled her waist. She wore almost no makeup, looked gorgeous, and knew it.

She pulled out her cell phone and speed-dialed a number. When the line was answered, she spoke briefly. "I've got a bunch of stuff from your designated group. They let out a whole lot of gas. They didn't name any names, but for sure it's your pair they're after. The Chinese are in it too. I'll encrypt it and send it to your phone."

At the other end of the line a lovely, athletic-looking brown-haired woman in her late twenties held a cell phone and a violin bow in one hand, and a very old, very valuable violin in the other. She wore a plain light-blue dress, no shoes, and her hair hung loosely just past her shoulders. She bore an uncanny resemblance to actress Amanda Crew. "Thanks, Gwen. I'll take a look at it right away. Please keep it up and be as careful as you can. Might be a good idea to not let 'em see you. They might get spooked if they find out you record stuff all the time. I think those guys are playing nasty. I'm leaving DC in a day or two, but I'll keep a watch on my messages."

"Travel safely, and watch your tail."

Sally Foarth ended the call on her cell phone, put it down, and continued practicing on the Guarneri del Gesu violin. She played Bach's Concerto for Violin in E Major, and then played Bach's Chaconne. She played these about as well as Kogan played them, several decades earlier. She was exceptionally gifted, had been a child prodigy, and at twenty-eight was at the top of her career as a performing violin soloist. She lived near her boyfriend Rico Morgan in east Idaho.

What Rico didn't know was that Sally Foarth was also an NSA agent. She used her international connections as a violinist to get information on people and politics in countries of interest to certain branches of the U.S. government. When she and Rico were at that post-concert reception in Montana Sally heard more than Rico, so she followed up on her own with a careful watch in the halls of Washington, DC. When she left Rico for her upcoming concert series in England she flew to DC instead of going directly to London, which she normally did anyway. She always told Rico she had to start in DC to make sure her visas and passport were in proper order, and to guarantee the delivery of her extremely valuable instrument into and back out of whatever country she visited. That made it easy for her to check with NSA Headquarters to see what might be asked of her on her next trip overseas.

Sally suspected her boyfriend Rico was targeted because he overheard the senators talking at that concert in Missoula. Her suspicions were aroused further when Rico told her his phone had been tapped before his trip to Las Cruces. She decided to see what she could find out. When she arrived in Washington she met with Gwen Fairbanks, her old friend who was head of local audio collection and internal surveillance for the Washington, DC, area for a branch of the NSA.

"Gwen," Sally said, "I'd like to put a bug on Senator Likkaman, the gay old boy from out West. I think he's into something he ought not to be doing. Can you implement that for me?"

"Consider it done, Sally. But what do you want, exactly? All his conversations, phone calls, anyone in particular he might meet up with?"

"Anyone who looks like Far Eastern, Chinese, Thai, or even Middle-Eastern, that sort of thing. I saw him with a younger oriental man who I believe was not gay, so what's that all about. Also, in Montana a while back I overheard him talking with one of his buddies about dead Mexicans, or maybe just dead bodies. Might be connected with the road project going on there, and importing Mexican workers along with some trick Mexi folding toilets, but I doubt it. So yes, Chinese, Middle and Far Eastern, and also anything he has to do with, or say to Senator Grafter. Grafter was in Montana with Likkaman."

"That old fart? What's he doing messing with the cowboy fag?"

"We'll have to wait and find out, I guess. My boyfriend Rico told me he was shot at recently and I want to see if I can find out what's behind all that."

"Can do, Sal. When do you leave for London?"

BORDER CAPER

"My concert series starts in four days. I'll fly out day after tomorrow, and I oughta be back ten days later. Please let me know if you catch any good stuff, Gwen."

"I'll call you, Sally."

Less than a day later Gwen struck pay dirt, phoned Sally, and sent her the coded and recorded message.

Now, from Gwen's just-gathered information Sally knew it was indeed the senators who were behind the attacks on Rico. She wanted to tell him, but could not do so without Rico wondering exactly how she found out, and that would 'blow her cover.' She hated that term. She had some idea why the senators were after Rico: They thought he heard them discussing dead Mexicans, knew he was an investigator, and didn't want him to find out anything more about their involvement, whatever it actually was. She knew now they had discussed the disposal of excess bodies but, oddly, there were no excess bodies. There were only those two Mexican girls killed within the last few months. Sally couldn't begin to guess how, or if, the senators were connected to that double murder. "Why in hell are these punk congressmen so concerned about excess bodies? What excess bodies? How's that Chinese guy fit in? After all, all we heard was some loose talk up there after the concert, and that's no reason to put a hit on Rico."

Later that same day Sally spotted her friend Roxy Roades as she walked down a hall in another Washington, DC, building toward the cafeteria. "Hi, Roxy! How'd that job out west go?"

"Sally, hi! As a matter of fact it was a complete bust. A real disaster, in fact. My people seem to have. . . *misled* me." This last sentence Roxy spoke in a low voice. The slender blonde gave a slight twist which sent her off-white skirt fanning out, showing her legs to a passing young male intern who nearly broke his neck turning to look at them.

"Oh?" Sally feigned more interest than she felt in the activities of her friend. Roxy Roades was from another agency, but you never know, Sally told herself, what information just might be important. Sally knew Roxy only in Washington, DC, and had never told Roxy her boyfriend was Rico Morgan. Sally walked down the hall with Roxy to the cafeteria. They found a corner table free of people, which gave them a chance to talk openly over coffee. 'What do you mean, misled you?"

"My office here in DC told me to go to El Paso airport and find a guy I'll call 'Joe.' When I got there I found Joe all right. Normally I'd have contacted the agency in El Paso but this was supposed to be a rush thing and I didn't have time to talk to anyone but this Joe. I had his photo from the agency in DC and he had a photo of me, and we found each other right off. So I knew he was the guy the agency wanted me to find. This Joe gave me a tracking scanner and told me to drive toward Las Cruces about twenty miles and stop on the highway, and then watch for a specific car. This is on the highway from El Paso to Las Cruces, the only road there, in fact. The car I was supposed to find was an ancient green Chevy that Joe had tagged with a GPS chip, so if I saw the old Chevy coming down the highway on the tracking scanner I was supposed to stop it somehow and call a number Joe gave me "

Now she had Sally's undivided attention. Sally knew all about Modesto's hot-rodded old green Chevy. Could it have been his?

Roxy continued her tale of woe. "The guy in the car I was stopping was said to be an imposter with some sort of key knowledge about drugs, or border crossings, or something else coming in across the border, and we needed to find out exactly who he was and what he knew. As I said, my job was to detain him and contact Joe, and he'd come with a team and take the imposter along for questioning. Stopping him on the highway would be safer than anywhere else because he was supposedly armed. That's what I was told. But when I stopped the car on the highway it turned out he wasn't an imposter after all. He was the real 'Joe.' He had proper photo ID, gave me the name of the local sheriff who knew him, stuff like that. There was another guy with him, and no sooner did I find out the guy in the car was who he claimed to be when along comes a chopper with bullets flyin'...."

"What! Good God. What did you do? A chopper...helicopter, you say, shooting at you?"

"Yes, someone tried to gun us down from a helicopter. This guy and his buddy pretty much saved my ass. They shot the gunner in the helicopter, and then we got the hell outa there. Man did that old Chevy move! I had to leave the rental car on the road. What a frickin' mess."

Rico had not told Sally anything about any shooting, nor anything about helping a sexy blonde on the highway. "Wow," she said. "That's not good at all. Obviously someone lied to you. Any idea when that started?"

"The whole thing came about from some western senator," Roxy continued. "He supposedly had info on this guy that the make-believe Joe was supposed to stop and it was a hurry-up deal. But now it looks to me like they wanted to get rid of the real Joe. My control here in DC told me about the senator's rush job before I ever left for El Paso, but I don't know which senator was involved. I guess my main office is plenty pissed at that senator now."

Sally was pretty sure she could name him, but kept quiet.

"So it looks like this guy on the highway was supposed to get whacked. But then it was me getting whacked along with him, and no one told me that. Those two guys were just too good for the helicopter guy, which is great or I might not be here now." Roxy was still upset about the whole episode, and justifiably so, as Sally could understand.

Roxy continued. "When we got to Las Cruces I contacted my El Paso office and asked about that guy Joe the agency had sent me to meet at El Paso airport. They had heard of Joe but knew nothing about any meeting or plan to stop some bogus guy who had info on border crossings. So the whole thing was bogus. I was set up before I ever left DC and I'm plenty pissed about it. No one seems to be able to tell me anything. That's the pisser of these spy agencies. Nobody trusts nobody." Roxy sipped her coffee, put down the cup and declared, "The screwiest thing is, as I said, the guy I stopped on the highway turned out to be the real 'Joe' that the guy at the airport had claimed to be. That means the El Paso 'Joe' was the only imposter in the whole deal. So, who the hell was that guy, the phony Joe, who gave me the GPS tracker? And why doesn't my agency tell me who told them to send me there? Why me?"

"What'd your El Paso contact say about the photo of the phony 'Joe'?"

"They told me they'd never seen him before...but I hope I see him again. The DC office now of course tells me the guy I met at the airport was a phony, which they conveniently found out after the fact. You'd think they'd check on this shit before sending a field agent out."

Sally knew the two guys on the road had been Rico and Modesto, but like Roxy or any good operative she wouldn't mention any names. Sally also could not ask any specific questions, but she realized she needed to alert Rico. He needed to know, she thought, that what he thought were potties were in fact bodies. He needed some clues damned fast because that might save him some terminal grief.

"So how'd you stop their car?" Sally sipped her coffee.

"I set my car on fire and showed 'em my tits," said Roxy.

Sally's mouthful of coffee landed on her skirt.

CHAPTER 6
Mexico

Rico and Modesto got off the airplane in the northern-Mexico city of Chihuahua, and Modesto Pincata Buena hailed a cab and gave the driver an address. No one bothered the duo during the trip to the unassuming small office building just off a busy street near the city's town hall. The receptionist spoke with Mole in Spanish and they were ushered into a small office just off the lobby.

There was strong light coming in from a tall frosted window next to the desk, and a ceiling fan spun lazily ten feet overhead. There was a slight smell of cigar smoke, probably lingering in the thick red carpeting, thought Rico. The walls were richly covered in dark oak paneling, and a tall set of oak bookshelves covered much of the wall behind the desk. They were half filled with law books, texts on politics, a row of novels in three languages, and some American books on firearms. Rico spotted the latest edition of *Cartridges of the World* in easy reach of the desk, along with a few back issues of *American Rifleman*, and a copy of *The Alaskan Retreater's Notebook* by Ray Ordorica.

BORDER CAPER

The remainder of the spaces on the shelves held diverse odds and ends, most of them heavy to help keep the books in place. One was a large rock flecked with what looked like gold. Another book-stopper was an ancient flintlock pistol mounted on a stone base. An old but still usable heavy brass Leitz microscope held sway near the end of another shelf. The instrument had a soft plastic cover over it. A Hallicrafters S-40A short-wave radio receiver was on a low shelf handy to the desk. A mandolin case stood on another shelf on the other side of the desk. A violin case rested near the mandolin, and a slightly battered guitar case stood in the corner near the window. A Paracho-made, peg-tuned flamenco guitar hung without case on the wall.

The air was cool, though the temperature outside had been in the mid-80s. A slight hum gave away the forced-air cooling and ventilation system. The slow ceiling fan kept the air in the room moving slightly. The thick door closed with a heavy thud behind the two visitors.

"Sound deadening, Eddie?" Rico asked the large, well-preserved man sitting at the desk.

"*Claro que sí*, Rico. It keeps all of my rude noises to myself." Eduardo 'Eddie' Mendoza got up, beaming, gave them each an *abrazo* and shook their hands warmly. "Welcome to Mexico, *amigos*!" Eddie spoke perfect English. On the surface, he was a key member of the Chihuahua branch of the Centro de Investigación y Seguridad Nacional (CISEN), which loosely translates into the Center for Research and National Security. He was also the U.S. CIA section head for that city. Eduardo went to college with Rico and Mole at the University of Michigan in Ann Arbor. Rico was studying Mechanical Engineering, Eduardo was in Law, and the Mole was, for a short time, in Literature, Science and the Arts. They got together at various bluegrass gatherings, drank coffee or cappuccino outdoors at Dominick's, ate at the old Brown Jug, drank the cheap red wine they bought by the gallon, played music together many times, and became fast friends while solving all the world's problems — the standard extracurricular task of all college students throughout the world. After Eduardo moved back to Mexico, Modesto to Las Cruces, and Rico to Colorado, the three stayed in touch. Eddie was a distant cousin of Modesto Pincata Buena.

"Eddie, how have you been," asked Rico. "You don't look a day over a hundred, *amigo*."

"Ah, always the kind word, eh? How about you, Mole, or is it *móle*? Have you lost weight?"

"*Pues, Eduardo, es verdad.* It's the truth. I've dropped one or two ounces: I trimmed my hair this morning. An' I don't touch that *móle* stuff. Not unless my *abuela* makes it, and she's dead."

"*Pues*, instead of *móle*, would you fellows care for a cigar? I have the Mexican Excelsiors or some Cuban Partagás, your choice."

"Thank you, *Don* Eduardo," said Rico. "I'll pop for a Cubanito, *por favor, y muchas gracias.*"

Modesto chose the milder Excelsior brand. Their cigars going nicely, the men's talk turned to reminiscences of old times at the U. of M., the friends they knew, the girls, the parties, the motorcycles, and more. Eddie asked, "Hey, what ever became of that buddy of yours with the pipe organ in his living room, the one you called EB?" Rico told him Steve Eberbach had invented the best speakers the world has ever seen, got married, and moved on to a better house...without the pipe organ.

"Do you remember...." And on they chatted, discussing people and events that happened when the three had shared life in the quiet college town in southern Michigan. They eventually came around to a discussion of bluegrass music, which they used to play together in Ann Arbor.

Eduardo put down his cigar, gave a big smile and said, "Amigos, how about we make some music, eh? Modesto, *mi guitarra es su guitarra.* I've been waiting for you guys! Let's do 'Red-Haired Boy!' Or like you renamed it, Rico, 'Ron Weasley!' But now you better call it 'Ed Sheeran,' my friend!" Eduardo reached for the violin and mandolin cases as Mole went to the guitar case near the window. Mole extracted a 1955 Martin D28 in immaculate condition, with a suitable pick intertwined in the strings. Eduardo handed the mandolin case to Rico and opened the violin case for himself. Rico pulled an old Gibson A-50 mandolin out. They all checked the tuning, which didn't take long because in anticipation of the meeting Eduardo had already made sure the instruments were ready to go.

The violin began the haunting, tricky sounds of the ancient fiddle tune, and the mandolin and guitar picked it up in turn. Each player took turns soloing on the theme, with the other two backing it or harmonizing. The small room was soon filled to overflowing with the bright, clear sound of bluegrass music. The three men played 'Whiskey Before Breakfast,' and then went right into 'Blackberry Blossom.' They added a few old Mexican songs to the mix, and to the delight of the other men, Eduardo grabbed the guitar and in a lilting tenor voice sang the ancient Venezuelan anthem '*Alma Llanera.*' After nearly an hour of exhaustive playing, they called a halt.

"My friends, that was some great pickin'," spoke Eduardo. "I can't thank you enough for indulging me. It's impossible to find anyone around here who knows these old tunes, much less can play them. All they want to do is play *'Guadalajara'* until the cows come home. But let's have some refreshments, and then we can discuss what it is you came down here for. Yes, Rico, when you phoned me two days ago, I know it was not to come here to make music."

He pressed a button on the corner of his desk, and in a few minutes a girl wheeled in a cart with a fairly hefty late lunch, common in that part of the world. After lunch the men relit their forgotten cigars, drank coffee, and got down to business.

Rico spoke directly and to the point, as he watched the cigar smoke get sucked into the overhead filtration unit. "Eddie, what do you know about the drug traffic across the border into New Mexico?"

"There's a lot of it, my friend, and it can't be stopped. The drug cartels have *soldados* by the thousand, if not by the ten thousand, and they make sure anyone going across the border to work carries some drugs across. It's easy. The *soldados* tell the migrant workers if they want to go across they've got to carry drugs. On the U.S. side, the border keepers, or U.S.-side *coyotes* — the guys watching the crossings and telling the *peones* where to go to get work — gather up the drugs as payment, and then a collector comes around maybe once a week and brings all the drug plunder to a central point, from which it goes out to every state in your country. All the shipments across the border are carefully accounted for, with an accounting system better than UPS uses, to make sure nothing gets stolen."

Eduardo continued. "The drugs come in from everywhere. Many tons of all kinds of drugs come from China, Burma and Thailand, and the rest of the Golden Triangle export some, and also provide some of the China supply. Southwest Asia, specifically Afghanistan, is a major source for heroin, but not a lot of that comes through Mexico.

"Mexico is an increasing producer of heroin over the past few years. Five years ago Mexico produced maybe five tons, metric tons, of it a year, but production has gone up since then. Mexico is the source of the so-called brown-powder heroin that's showing up increasingly in eastern United States cities, like Chicago, Detroit, and even in New York. Mexico produced maybe eight or ten tons of heroin last year. Afghanistan produced about five *hundred* tons. Cocaine comes in from Colombia, Brazil and Venezuela, and from Bolivia and Peru. Every year about a thousand to twelve-hundred tons of cocaine is shipped out of South America."

"Holy shit!" said Rico. "I had no idea of the volume!" Mole just whistled.

Eduardo continued. "Mostly, Mexico is simply the pipeline for drugs coming from the far East and from South America into the United States. The U.S. is the biggest consumer of all kinds of illegal drugs in the world, so that's the destination of choice. Remember, my friends, cocaine has a price of about $30,000 a kilo in the U.S. So now you can better understand the wars for control of drug-trafficking territories in Mexico, and the unbelievable brutality that goes with it. With that kind of money, human life means absolutely nothing to these traffickers. The other pipeline to the U.S. is of course Canada, but border crossing there is neither so easy nor so comfortable year-around as the southern border. There are not a whole lot of Canadians who want to go pick oranges in the U.S. for their life's work.

"The main thing is to understand that drugs and people move constantly from Mexico to the U.S. Your country's open-door policy is encouraged by your government because every time drugs and people come in, money and guns move south. This helps the shadow government implement its program of corrupting the heart of your country, and makes lots of money for the industries that both run Washington, DC, and also deal in the weapons that move south of your border. Some of that might change if your Democratic party lets the Trump administration get its wall, but I seriously doubt it. One way or another, wall or no, the drugs will get to your country.

Eddie drew on his cigar, blew smoke at the ceiling, and went on, "This guns-for-drugs trade generally involves the CIA working in conjunction with several far-eastern countries, like China, both Koreas and the Philippines, to move old surplus U.S.-made weapons like M14s and of course the lusted-after AK-47s into the hands of the Mexican drug cartels, and the hands of the South-American ones as well. And of course the U.S. gangs steal all the guns they can, and send them to Mexico in payment for more drugs. All in all it's an enormous mess, and it can't be stopped. And some people wonder why the CIA doesn't want a wall built along the Mexican border."

"That's a lot of information," spoke Rico, "way more than I expected, actually. I had some idea of the scope of drug traffic, but I had no concept of the volume."

Modesto asked, "Do the cartels use specific areas of New Mexico regularly? Or is the cross-border trafficking a hit-or-miss operation?"

"The drug movers use everything at their disposal to get the stuff out of Mexico and into the U.S. wherever there's an easy way to move it," answered Eduardo, puffing on his Partagás. "They move it by land, sea, underground, under water, and by air. If there's an unguarded hole somewhere in the border of New Mexico or Arizona or California or Texas, you can count on drugs coming through that hole. Drugs come in through Mississippi, Louisiana and Florida to some extent, too. A lot of it of course moves in with the Mexican migrant workers. It even comes in with the pregnant women who want to have their babies in the U.S. for guaranteed citizenship, free medical care, even free prenatal care for their kids. These women are more than happy to make all kinds of sacrifices to get across the border. You can bet they bring drugs with them. Unfortunately, they are the little ones, and the ones who generally get caught and thrown in jail for trafficking. They're the desperate pregnant women and some of the relatively innocent men who themselves are desperate to make some money north of the border. The big drug jockeys seldom get caught. They're more likely to get shot in a border war."

Rico pondered his cigar a while. Then he spoke carefully. "Eduardo, our big problem, the real reason we're here, is the pregnant women. They seem to be getting cut up for their babies, which we don't understand. Are the drug shipments inserted into the females' wombs, do you know, or are their bellies just full of kids?"

Mole said, "Eddie, in the case of a murdered Mexican woman in Chicago, the forensic examination seemed to rule out her having drugs in the womb, but maybe you know better. Several parcels of drugs were found in the woman's handbag, a few thousand dollars worth in fact, but that was somewhat less than the normal amount for someone to have carried across the border. But no one knows how she got to Chicago."

"*Amigos*," said Eduardo, "I don't think the drugs are primarily put inside the women. That's fairly dangerous, and no one wants to deal with that sort of thing on a regular basis. It's too messy. I believe the drugs are simply put into a heavy plastic bag that can be left in the desert if need be, or dropped on the roadside for later recovery, especially if the bags have a marker chip in the bag so they can be found electronically."

"That's kind of uptown, isn't it."

"What do you mean?"

Rico sipped his coffee. "It's higher tech than I would have expected from some *banditos* who can hardly find their ass with both hands. But I guess if there's big money to be made, there's people who can make that high-tech stuff affordable, accessible, and easy enough to use, for everyone involved."

"Heck, they could just put a cell phone in the bag. They all have GPS trackers in 'em now. Of course," continued Eduardo, "a few poor fools are talked or forced into swallowing plastic bags full of drugs to be passed out later, but every TV-cop show since the dawn of time has had an episode where one of the bags burst and killed the guy. So everyone knows about it, no one wants to do it, and on top of that the cops are watching for strange trips to the toilet at border crossings."

Mole was sitting back, smoking silently for much of this exchange, but then he sat up and asked, "What about small aircraft? Are they used much to carry drugs?"

"Yes, certainly. Small, big, you name it. Don't forget that Air Force C-130 that landed in Florida a few years ago, with something like 20 tons of cocaine in it, presumably 'to be destroyed.' " He made quote marks in the air with his fingers. "The money in drugs makes it possible for the dealers to buy a large airplane, fill it with drugs, fly it to the U.S., unload the drugs, and then completely abandon the airplane. That 20 tons of cocaine had a street value of half a *billion* dollars. With small aircraft, one method is to fly low at night and drop shipments to a contact on the ground with some kind of light signals. Sometimes they try it in the daylight, a little Cessna 150 flying 20 feet off the deck, looking for a marker, something like three small red tarps in a line, or a blue and red tent set up somewhere, you get the idea. The pilot tosses out the package and he's gone across the border again. How are you going to stop someone like that? Bring in an Apache chopper at a million dollars a second to stop a drop of five or ten pounds of cocaine? Hardly. So the druggers win again."

"What about distribution after the drugs get across the border?" Rico asked.

Eddie continued his narrative. "The gangs all along the border, on both sides, generally handle that. Prime among them is MS-13, the Mara Salvatrucha, a brutal and organized bunch of goons that are part of the drug wars down here, fighting for control of the distribution lines or paths. They have from 30,000 to 50,000 members worldwide, maybe 10,000 in the U.S. in all major cities."

Mole asked, "They're South Americans, aren't they?"

"*Claro*," said Eduardo," most of them. They came out of El Salvador after the civil war there, came into L.A., and just grew. They're well armed, and know how to use their guns too."

Mole asked, "Would they be involved with stealing babies?"

"They're brutal," Eduardo replied, "but I can't see them doing that for any good reason. How many women have been cut open?"

Mole replied, "So far as we know there have been six separate incidents involving eight women. Probably more. Most of them happened in New Mexico, but at least one and possibly several more were in Chicago. One woman was found badly decomposed in Lake Michigan north of Chicago, but forensics were not sure the woman had lost her baby to butchers or to the fishes."

"*Amigos*, I will put out some feelers, but I think your problem is not solely related to drugs."

Rico and Mole shook hands with their old friend, and the duo took their leave.

Back at the hotel they put their heads together about it. Mole said, "Rico, I don't believe we're on the right track down here. I can't see a clear connection between drugs and babies."

"I agree. If we follow the money, there's nothing in it for the drug gangs to try to sell unborn babies, alive or dead. Which means we had a nice vacation in the sun for not much of anything."

"Speak for yourself, amigo, I have a date tonight with Eddie's hostess."

The next morning Rico knocked on the door to Mole's room with two cups of coffee. When bleary-eyed Mole finally opened the door, Rico said, "Hey, amigo, don't tell me about your hot date. We don't have time. We have to hit the road to go visit someone else today."

Modesto Pincata Buena groggily shook his head and took a big slug of the coffee. "Now what? More information about the drug trade? Please tell me no."

"We're going to visit a man who had ties to one of the dead girls. He's her uncle, in fact, or so I found out from Eduardo this morning. The Las Cruces cops found some letters, and they mentioned this guy. Eddie set it up for us. It's just a short drive north, and you can sleep on the road if you wish."

They hit the road and after getting lost twice, found the right road out of the city, into the gently rolling hills just outside Chihuahua. Mole dozed while Rico drove the rental car north past what appeared to be farmland, on into the somewhat barren country higher in the hills. After a short while, there were only sparse signs of civilization, but finally they rounded a corner and came upon their destination.

The *estancia* or ranch house of Juan Cordota y Carazco was, on the outside, not very imposing. The house was surrounded by a high wall that kept snoopers out, and if a determined intruder were to attempt to cross the wall he would find broken glass set into the concrete on top of the wall, the standard low-key security seen throughout much of Mexico — as it has been for many generations. Inside the wall there was a grassy space all around the house, separating the house from the wall on all sides by fifty yards or more. To the uninitiated it looked like a pleasant private dwelling, but when Rico and Mole saw it, they both said the same thing: "Fortress."

Access through the outer wall was through a gate attended by a fit-looking young man who had an intercom link to the main house. The house had several narrow windows on the ground floor, with one large one overlooking the front of the house. The upper story was nearly windowless, but both men observed the gun slits on that floor. Anyone in the yard would be vulnerable to rifle fire from the upper floor of the house. The front entrance to the house led down a short passage, the walls of which also had slits on the side, so the door could only be approached by passing the observation ports. The house was set up to be easily defensible from almost any attack short of a missile.

Rico's friend Eddie had set up the interview with Cordota, so Rico and his friend were expected. Properly identified, they drove through the iron gate and parked near the front door. Another fit-looking man acted as the butler and led them indoors, down a long hall, and into a high-ceilinged room decorated with some bright red and white tapestries. What appeared to be an excellent copy of a not-well-known Van Gogh hung on one wall. Two small fine-wood tables, several comfortable-looking padded chairs, and a large desk were the only furniture items in the room. On the desk were a computer screen, a corded pushbutton telephone, a pad of paper, a pen, and nothing else. As they entered the room, *Don* Cordota, a short, athletic-looking man with a hard-looking face rose and came around the desk to greet them. He spoke slightly accented English.

Mole had not been talkative on the trip out, but as soon as he laid eyes on Cordota he fell completely silent.

"*Señor* Cordota," said Rico, "I am extremely sorry for the recent loss of your niece. I know that might sound hollow, but I will do everything in my power to bring the perpetrators of the crime to justice. I was informed her remains are being sent back here for burial. If there is anything I can do for you please don't hesitate to ask."

"What are you, *Señor* Morgan? Some kind of cop?" Cordota's gaze was cold and penetrating. He reminded Rico of Lee Van Cleef, and he looked like he hadn't smiled for several decades. He wore a white shirt open at the neck, no jacket, and dress slacks of a dark blue color.

"I'm a private investigator, though presently I am pursuing a series of murders largely on my own ticket, but with the blessings of the United States Department of Immigration Enforcement. My associate *Señor* Pincata Buena asked me if I would help him look into the murders. I met him in Las Cruces, and we suddenly found ourselves to be the center of attention of those who would kill us. Several attempts have been made on each of us. But we don't know why, and frankly, we're getting tired of getting shot at. I suspect we know something we are not aware of, and my purpose in visiting Mexico, and you, is to find out all I can about these murders, find out why people are trying to kill us, why they killed your niece, see if there's a link to the drug trafficking, and to discover anything that might tie all these rather strange and most unwelcome events together."

"And how do you think I might be able to help you?"

"Your niece had your name among her belongings. We presume she was going to the U.S. to have her baby and bring it up as a U.S. citizen. I thought you might be able to give us some background information on her, such as who the father might be, who were her friends here in Mexico, what sort of a life she had, and anything else that might help us find out why she was attacked. She and her friend were found with traces of drugs on them. We suspect the two girls had entered the country illegally, and probably were forced to carry drugs as part of the deal. No significant quantity of drugs was found and none of it was in their bloodstreams. We believe there was no reason to kill the girls to steal the drugs. The only reason for the killings seems to have been to take their unborn babies. I have no interest nor intent of pursuing this investigation from the standpoint of illegal drugs. I believe something more important is at stake, something worth far more than money."

Juan Cordota sat quietly for quite some time, looking at nothing. Rico glanced at Mole, who was still saying nothing. He was staring at the rug, keeping his eyes lowered all the time. Rico thought he saw a flicker of something odd in Mole's eye.

Finally, Cordota said, "*Señor* Morgan, my niece was not my niece. She was in fact my housekeeper, and also my lover. I was the father of her baby. If you can help in any way to find the people who did this to her, I will forever be in your debt. Of course I will check up on what you have told me about your background, though I expect you are telling the truth. Otherwise you would not be here. My story is short...."

Cordota told Rico and Mole the story of the girl who needed funds, and wanted to have a baby in the U.S. There was not a lot to tell, but Rico sensed that Cordota had strong feelings for the girl, much stronger than he was letting on in his short and sad tale.

"And that is all I have to tell you, *Señor* Morgan. Do you have any information you can share with me?"

"*Señor* Cordota, about the only thing we've determined so far is that someone on this side of the border must have informed the killers these two girls were coming. Their stage of pregnancy, which followed the general pattern of the other murders, and the fact that the two girls were essentially alone could have triggered the attack. The babies had to be at the right stage of development and the girls had to be vulnerable. The most likely person to know that and be able to alert the killers would be one of the border-guides, or *coyotes*, as they're called. He would have had time to evaluate the two before they crossed, maybe question them about how far along they were in their pregnancies, and make sure no one else capable of making a threat, such as a sturdy man, was crossing with them. Then he'd made a call to alert the murderers. But we have yet to determine just who it was that was alerted."

After another minute's silence, Cordota said, "That is good logic, Mr. Morgan. In my grief I had failed to think this through, and your information and reasoning bring light to the situation. Now, then, there is something you might want to look into. The only thing more valuable than drugs is life itself, and as soon as I knew the babies had been removed, I was reminded of something I saw a few years ago in a report in some big American magazine. And that is stem-cell research."

Rico's eyes narrowed and hardened as he gazed into the razor-sharp visage of Juan Cordota. The interview was over. The Mexican man waved his hand and his "butler" appeared as by magic to escort the two men back out into the hot Mexican sunshine.

BORDER CAPER

On the drive back to the Chihuahua airport neither man said much of anything for a while. Finally Mole sighed deeply and said softly to Rico, "Do you know who that man is, my friend?"

Rico pondered that for a long time. Finally he said, "Clearly he has money and some great degree of importance in this barren part of the world. I suppose he's some sort of retired head of industry, or maybe a politician, as a guess."

"You might say he's a kind of head of an industry. I have never heard this man's name, but have seen his face several times in photos. He is the overlord of about one-third the total drug traffic from Mexico to the United States. He commands an army of at least a thousand men in his sordid business, and is one of the wealthiest and most dangerous men in the world. As soon as I saw his face I recognized him. Frankly, my friend, I was scared shitless to be in the same room with him. Did you see that Van Gogh? It was not a reproduction."

"Oh, come on. You must be mistaken. He was polite, obviously in love with the poor girl who was killed, and was above all a gentleman. He had a good command of English, and had enough presence to not go weeping in front of us. How could he be what you say?"

"My friend, I am most emphatically not mistaken. If I were connected with the death of that girl and knew who the father was, I would take myself off to the Moon, or Mars, because nowhere on earth would I feel safe."

When he was once again alone, Juan Cordota Carazco sat thinking for a long time. Finally he picked up his telephone and dialed a number that rang in a little house near the saloon where the *coyote* Ramón Sapresta had taken the two girls shortly before they crossed. He spoke with one of his "soldiers" in low tones for a short while. Then he said "Bring him. Bring

Ramón." and hung up. A slight smile touched his hawk-like face, and it was not a smile of joy.

When Rico finally reached his home in Idaho he phoned Sally who was still in DC. After the usual pleasantries he asked, "Sally, do you happen to know anything about stem cells?"

"All I know is what you can dig out of Wikipedia, but they're not telling it all. I think some of the most potent ones come from aborted fetuses, but there's also something to do with bone marrow for transplants and the like. Other'n that, I know zip."

"Well, dear, if you happen to hear of any, let's say, advanced stem-cell research, let me know. It might have to do with the case I'm working on."

"The cut-up pregnant girls? I don't think so. Their babies were too far along to have much value for the early, most-potent stem cells."

"What! Are you sure?"

"That's what I've read. The most useful stem cells come from early stages of fetus development."

"Oh." Rico pondered that information. "Well, crap! Then that's a dead end. When do you leave for England?"

"Tomorrow." She paused. "Rico, I'm glad you called, and that you're all right. I suspected you might've had a worse time in New Mexico than you told me. Promise me you'll be careful when I'm gone. As you say, check your six, and be sure to check your seven and eight too!"

"I'll even check my nine and ten for you, dear. Are you all set for your flight?"

"Pretty much, but I'm worried about what I'd do with the potties of you and Mole if anything happened to you. Where would I bury them?"

94

"The what?" Rico asked.

"Er, the *bodies.* What'd I say?"

"I dunno but it wasn't bodies. Look, nothing is going to happen to us. I won't let it happen. Just go play good fiddle and don't worry. When will I see you again?"

"In about two weeks. I'll email you."

He wished her well and they said goodbye. After she broke the connection Sally Foarth asked herself, "Will he get it? I hope he gets it."

Rico hung up his land line, poured himself a stiff Balvenie on ice, and stared at the wall for a long time.

CHAPTER 7
Wing

"**D**amn! How did Heifetz get those octaves so easily?" Sally Foarth asked a rhetorical question of herself. She had just performed a solo rendition of Bach's Chaconne for a full house at The Royal Festival Hall in London as a conclusion to her night's performance with the London Philharmonic, and although she played it well, she failed to play one note in the massive work that no one in the audience had caught, but which left her sorely embarrassed. The legendary Jascha Heifetz had made the work look extremely easy as he performed it on a video Sally downloaded off the Internet, and studied hard, apparently to little avail as she now told herself. She was not about to concede that Heifetz was better than she was, although in her heart of hearts she had to agree with her boyfriend Rico Morgan that Heifetz had been the all-time master of the violin. She realized Heifetz had a Russian — actually Lithuanian — sensuality or passion to his playing, particularly noticeable on the Bach pieces, that even Leonid Kogan couldn't quite match, but she'd never admit to Rico that Rico was right, and that she admired Heifetz and Kogan as much as he did. She played up her admiration for a young Yehudi Menuhin, which gave her good arguing points with Rico, and so kept her true violinist's heart hidden.

But she had other matters at hand, and took her post-concert bows like a trouper, and then took her leave of the stage. She of course made her mandatory appearance at the post-concert gathering of local dignitaries, and for that occasion her escort was Sir Phillip Roscoe Hornsbury Beagle, third Earl of Chutney, a distinguished man of seventy years with a white mustache and puffy sideburns. He was also her British counterpart, her MI6 (SIS) contact.

As she entered the post-concert gathering on his arm, she asked him, "Tell me, Sir Phillip, what news do you have that might be of interest to me?" Sally had known him for over a decade, since she had first come to London for advanced violin studies. Sir Phillip's niece was Sally's tutor's wife. The intelligence contact had been established five years after they had met, to the surprise and delight of both the old man and the young woman.

"Silver's up. So's gold." The old man spoke with a cough and grumble, the effect of years of cigarette smoking. "But if you mean serious stuff, we can't stop the influx of talented violinists named Sally no matter what we do. They just keep coming to England, and they get better and better, or so it seems to my old ears."

"Why, thank you!" Sally blushed slightly. "You are too kind. I was off tonight, maybe because I have too much on my mind. I'm actually quite aware of bullion prices, having some holdings of my own, but I was hoping to get some insight into the recent illegal affairs of a certain far-Eastern country close to Taiwan. And not drugs. We know all about *that* unstoppable menace."

"Well, if you must talk Far-Eastern shop instead of Bach, I know that a certain Chinese man, Wun something, made contact with a pair of nasty Arabs some months ago, one of whom was recently killed in the United States. The Chinese fellow didn't much like that, I'm told. But I have no idea what the deal was — though I could guess. I suspect one of your elder senators might also be able to shed some light on that arrangement, albeit reluctantly."

"But are any countries in that region interested in, oh, say, advanced stem-cell research?" Sally asked. " I spoke with a guy I know just before I left the U.S. He asked me if I knew anything about it and I told him no, which was the truth. But he rang a bell in my head, so I'm asking you."

Sir Phillip paused for half a minute. "I do have a little direct knowledge of stem cell research by a particular country in the far East. As I understand stem cells, they come for the most part from unborn short-term fetuses close to the embryo stage, usually aborted ones in the scheme of things. A nasty business, that. The stem cells are capable of reproducing damaged organs, skin, bones, even teeth to some extent, and thus are most useful in helping to heal broken people. To what exact extent they can actually help, we're not all that knowledgeable, but we know there have been recent major advances in their use. Some of the most advanced uses have been reported in the scientific journals by a research team consisting of a German man and a Chinese woman working together in Hong Kong. And there's certain knowledge of cooperation between China and Germany in Hamburg as well. Most of this is very hush-hush. The reports are dashed vague, so I've been told."

He continued, "However, we do know of a Chinese oddity that springs to mind. Something of an anomaly in the scheme of things. A glitch, as it were, in the passage of time. This is a fellow whom you might wish to examine. He is indeed Chinese, and has a most curious aspect to his imperturbable, inscrutable countenance."

"I love it when you talk dirty," she said.

"He is all of seventy-three years old, a fact carefully vetted by our best men, yet he appears to be a good deal younger. More to the point, he acts it, having a lady friend who is twenty-six years old, athletically inclined, and currently his lover. He also runs several miles a day and seems to eat whatever he wants, including western foods and lots of steaks, near-raw meat. We've had our eye on him, but only as a curiosity. I don't know if this addresses your questions, or if stem-cell research might be part of it, but you might wish to look into it. His name is Wing, ah, Hung Lo, I believe, and he is currently visiting London. I can get you an introduction, if you like."

Sally asked, "And you suppose he might have some connection to the recent advances in stem cell research? Or does he just know a good plastic surgeon?"

"He is from Hong Kong, and unless he has found the fountain of youth we cannot explain his youthful activities in any other way. However, what we know of stem-cell therapy could not have produced what we are seeing in him. It must be either something entirely new or something deeply under cover. Of course he could have had plastic surgery, but that would not give him the stamina to permit him to, erm, perform with this young woman."

"I'd love to get a look at him, but perhaps not by knocking on his door. Could you arrange for me to sneak a peek without his knowing about it?"

"Nothing easier. Come with me."

Sir Phillip put her on his arm and walked across the crowded room, with here a nod to an acquaintance, and there an odd word to another. He stopped by a portal leading into another chamber of the building in which the post-concert gathering was being held, and positioned himself so that she could look out into the room behind him.

Sir Phillip leaned toward Sally. "Look along the wall to your right, to the painting of Bach hanging on the wall above the next doorway. Wing is the man in red, with the doxie on his arm."

Sally followed the directions with her eyes, and her gaze fell on a man in a red oriental formal jacket and contrasting scarf. There was a stunning blonde on his arm. She wore a simple black evening gown that, as Sally could see, belied its cost. "Oh!" She exclaimed. "I know her! That's Betsy Jackery, from the U.S. She moved here a few years ago. . .we used to be friends. How is she connected to the Chinese man?"

"I have no idea, but they have not been together all that long. Perhaps she brought Wing here, knowing something of your talent and wanting to impress him. Do you know her well? Because that could be inconvenient if you don't want to meet him."

"I used to know her well, but haven't seen her for the past few years. But I can't believe what I'm seeing. You say he's in his seventies?"

"He's seventy-three in fact," said Sir Phillip.

"But he looks about thirty. What the deuce! I'm going to have to get closer to him. I can't believe he's not just drastically made up."

"Let's go, then," said Sir Phillip. "I'll introduce you."

He led her on his arm slowly toward the Chinese man and the blonde American woman. The Chinese man was conversing with a distinguished-looking middle-aged man who Sir Phillip informed Sally was Sir Ovaren Dunwidth, a Member of Parliament. Betsy Jackery was trying to look interested, but her boredom was evident. Sally saw Betsy's face light up as they approached.

Betsy spoke first. "Sally! Hullo. I loved the concert!"

"Hello, Betsy. Nice to see you again." Sally noticed the Chinese man slowly turn toward her, and comprehend that he was indeed looking at the star of the evening's performance. Sally noted that though he looked young, and indeed had no facial wrinkles nor exterior signs of aging, he tended to behave and move as would an elderly man. His hair was dark brown, his eyes were clear and had no wrinkles in their corners, and when he smiled, he displayed what appeared to be perfect teeth with no traces of the staining of age.

Sir Phillip introduced Sally to Wing and the MP, and Sally did the same for Betsy to Sir Phillip. Sir Ovaren Dunwidth, the MP, congratulated Sally, made pleasant noises for a few moments, made his excuses, and left them.

"Ah, Miss Foarth, how lovely of you to honor us with your presence," spoke Wing Hung Lo. "You played the Chaconne much like I would have expected of Jascha Heifetz, which is to say, most brilliantly."

To herself Sally said, "And if you can tell Heifetz from Kogan or Perlman or Menuhin, I bet a nickel you caught that missed note, damn it."

Out loud she said, "Thank you. I am a great fan of Heifetz's, though most listeners tend to think I am more fond of Menuhin from my style of playing."

"Oh, no, I disagree," spoke Wing Hung Lo. "I am a great 'aficionado' of the violin and it's plain to my ear that you have Heifetz at heart, not Menuhin. Menuhin, like so many, drags the bow on the A-string instead of playing the full second chord of the Chaconne, which is of course incorrect, because by so doing he omits the notes that Bach wrote in the original score. Heifetz and Kogan and only a few other violinists, yourself included, play it correctly."

To herself again, "Sumbitch. If he knows that, and can hear that, can Rico tell the difference? Rico loves Heifetz, so I've always told him I'm a fan of Menuhin to get his goat. Does Rico *know*? How good is his ear for violin styles? Damn banjo picker!"

"Well, Mr. Wing, I confess, now you know my source. I am indeed a great follower of Heifetz, but please don't tell anyone. There's someone back home who must not find out my secret."

"My dear, your secret is safe with me," said Wing. "And please call me Hung."

"I bet you are," spoke Sally to her inner violinist, "but I hope I never find out."

She smiled, all the while marveling at the youthful complexion of the aged Chinese man. His skin was flexible, healthy-looking, even slightly tanned. There were no indications of plastic surgery either. Could he really be seventy-three? She decided to pry a bit, if he let her.

"Hung, because you are so good at telling the various violinists' styles, I must ask you if you play."

"Oh, I have a decent fiddle that I pick up from time to time. My brother and I often play duets. I have a Strad, but my brother prefers his Guarneri del Gesu, as you obviously do also. We do play a bit of Bach, because we admire him above all composers."

She thought, "So this old fucker has megabucks, eh?" She asked, "How long have you been playing?" she asked, gently prying again.

BORDER CAPER

"Miss Foarth, sometimes it seems like forever, and sometimes it seems like I picked up the violin just yesterday." He turned to his date Betsy. "My dear, I believe it's time for us to bid adieu to this fond gathering. Will you excuse us, Miss Foarth? Thank you again for a wonderful evening."

She thought, "That old fart didn't want to admit a thing. Maybe he doesn't want Betsy to know. I must ask her if she knows."

"Betsy, I must get your phone number! I'm in London for a few more days. Maybe we can do some shopping together." Sally held Betsy's arm gently.

"Oh, that'd be great," Betsy said. "Here." And she scratched it on the corner of her concert program. "My flat is near the Regal Hotel just off Piccadilly."

"I know that area. I'll phone you tomorrow." Sally watched Betsy and Wing depart.

"Sir Phillip," she said, "there's something wrong about that fellow. He's not quite all he's supposed to be."

"You noticed it, eh? Good. He's hiding something and we'd like to know what it is. He certainly didn't want to discuss his age, did he?"

"Not in the slightest. I plan to ask Betsy tomorrow on the phone if she knows his age. I bet she doesn't."

The next day Sally phoned Betsy and they arranged to meet for a shopping spree near Piccadilly Circus that afternoon. The women had a great time enjoying the early spring weather and becoming reacquainted. They met during college, and palled around for a season or two until Betsy moved to London a few years ago, following her boyfriend of the time. Betsy liked London, got a job and stayed, though the boyfriend hadn't lasted.

Sally visited her on one of her trips when she was ostensibly taking advanced violin training, but was actually on an NSA mission. This shopping trip was the first time they had been together in three years.

After buying a few things neither of them needed, they had coffee in a small shop. Sally wanted to know how much Betsy knew about the odd Chinese man.

"So, is Hung a good lover?" Sally blurted. "Is he really...hung?"

Besty giggled. "Hung is *quite* athletic, actually, which I guess you could tell from his physique."

"How old is he," asked Sally innocently.

"He told me he's in his forties, but he sure doesn't look it, does he?"

Sally thought to herself, "So the old boy has a lot to hide. But why?" She asked Betsy, "How did you meet?"

"We were both at a wine-tasting event. I was there with my brother, and Hung was with another Chinese fellow, and I believe Sir Ovaren Dunwidth, the MP, was there with them too. You met him last night. Hung introduced himself when he noticed I was caught up in the music of a string quartet there playing a Vivaldi piece. He asked if I enjoyed violin music and I of course told him I knew one of the finest violinists in the world."

"I didn't know you knew Itzhak Perlman," said Sally.

Betsy laughed. "Yes, I met ol' Itzhak in New York at one of your concerts," she quipped. She continued, "Hung told me you were going to play a concert at the Festival Hall in a fortnight and asked if I would like to attend with him. I told him I hardly knew him, so he invited me to dinner, I accepted, and we hit it off. That's pretty much the whole story up to right now."

"Does he have many friends in London? I mean, what's he doing here, if you don't mind my asking. He's clearly a Hong-Kong type fellow, if you get my drift.

"Yes, he's somewhat out of his element," answered Betsy, "and I think he'd be a lot more at home in a Chinese environment. But he told me he had to meet with some Members of Parliament, and some Arabs, or maybe Lithuanians, I'm not sure. So he had to come here for about a month, which means he'll be gone back to Hong Kong in about another week. But heck, it's been fun and he's treated me well, so I'm not complaining."

"Is he big on rice, or does he eat Western food when you go out? I know I'd be uncomfortable if my date whipped out a set of chopsticks over a bowl of noodles while I dug into roast duck across the table from him."

Betsy laughed. "He eats more meat than I do, and rare at that. I swear that guy could eat a whole cow if you cooked it up for him. He's definitely not a rice hound. I suspect his appetite for meat has to do with those insulin injections he gives himself every other day.

Sally's head reeled with this sudden news about the insulin injections. She had had a diabetic dog, and had to give the poor animal two injections every day. Insulin was most definitely not injected every other day, so far as Sally knew.

Sally said, "I thought insulin had to be taken every day, sometimes more than once a day."

"So did I, but this is supposed to be something new. It's a vile-looking blue liquid. He won't let me near it. Said it costs a bomb, and he couldn't risk spilling it. But enough about me and Hung. How's Rico doing? Are you still with him?"

Sally kept her thoughts about the injections to herself, and filled Betsy in on the latest available news about Rico Morgan, which was pretty much not much of anything. Sally knew Rico didn't like his criminal investigation stories to be told out of school, as it were, so she kept it innocent and low key.

"He's still pickin' the banjo, and it's a real kick to play fiddle tunes on the Guarneri with him. One time he said he never knew *Blackberry Blossom* could sound like a million bucks until he heard it on my fancy fiddle.

"He's had his pilot's license for a few years now, and he bought a small airplane, a Citabria, which is lots of fun for both of us. His dog is his best friend, not me. But that's okay because I can't be with him all the time. He needs someone to 'hound' him, if you'll pardon the pun."

The talk switched to old dates, old times, shared adventures, and finally wound down about dusk. The two parted, with promises to stay in touch.

Back at her room, Sally lost little time. She had to find out more about whatever it was the Chinese man was injecting into himself. She opened her cell phone and started to dial a number, thought better of it and used her encoder on the hotel's landline phone.

CHAPTER 8
Blue

On the scrambled landline Sally Foarth spoke with her NSA Chief of Staff, London, and explained her findings about the odd Chinese man and his blue liquid. "Sir, I believe we need to have a sample of that stuff. I understand he has about a dozen small bottles, like the kind insulin comes in. Any idea how to get some? Maybe he won't miss one bottle. . . ?"

"Sally, we'll take care of it," said the Chief. "We'll suck some into a needle so he won't miss any. And we'll get that done quickly, because you say he's leaving town soon. Thank you for your research." The line went dead. The response had been quick, clear, and professional. Nothing more was said, nor did it need to be said.

Sally picked up her violin and resumed her daily practice session.

Within a day a surreptitious visit had been made to the rented London flat of the odd Chinese man, and a sample of the blue liquid was secured. Such covert operations were one of the specialities of the London branch of the NSA, and as things transpired, Wing Hung Lo never knew of the loss of a small bit of his precious blue fluid.

The fluid was brought to a small but efficient laboratory in the south side of London, not far from the Thames. There it was given to a senior lab officer with the explicit instructions to perform qualitative and quantitative analyses of it to determine, as best as possible, what exactly it contained. The results were astounding to the elderly lab officer who performed the analysis.

He phoned the NSA Chief of Staff and told him what he had discovered. "Sir," said the lab chief, "that damned blue soup's alive. I swear it was looking back at me under the microscope! The blue cells appeared to be similar to embryonic stem cells, but they were swimming in a manner that indicated they were almost intelligent. I stuck a needle into the soup under the microscope, and the cells tried to get away from it. I have never seen anything like it in my life."

"Was this behaviour anything like normal stem cells?" the London Chief of Staff asked.

"No, sir. I've seen them and they are generally benign under observation, while still retaining their sense of life. These were much more aggressive. They were like stem cells on steroids. We're not sure yet what the other ingredients are, but they were positively of biological origin, and our best guess is they're of human origin. Per your suggestion we injected it into several mice, one of which was an older specimen. All the treated mice showed an increased tendency toward consuming raw meat, and the older mouse, normally quite peaceful, became aggressive towards the others. It was as if he were asserting himself like a much younger mouse."

After a pause on the phone, the Chief of Staff asked, "Did he show any other signs of age regression? Less gray, or anything?"

"Well, after a few hours he mounted one of the female mice, if that's what you're asking. It has not been long enough for his grayness to diminish. Only two days. However. . . ." The chief of the lab paused.

"Yes?"

"This makes me think hard about the work of DePinho at Harvard, with telomere shortening. In a nutshell, he gave mice an enzyme that prevented the telomeres — caps on the chromosomes — from being shortened, which reduced the signs of aging. It also brought aged mice back to some previous state of aging, approaching youth again. Some of the mice discussed in his papers showed similar signs to my mice here, though his enzyme took months to show the effects I'm seeing here in days. By the way, the Russians apparently have some new age-delaying pills that Putin looked at recently, but I don't know if that ties into this stuff. No one but the Russians knows their content."

"Thank you," said Chief, and abruptly hung up.

CHAPTER 9
Germany

Rico sat and sipped his Scotch and soda in a serious funk. What Sally told him several days ago about the use of stem cells from early-term unborn babies didn't jive with the removal of five-month-term babies. Rico spent his time since Sally left taking care of projects around his little ranch. He tried to get his mind off the murders, but it was impossible. He kept coming back to the potential uses for dead unborn children, but had no answers. He asked himself, again and again, "What are they using them for?" He had nothing to indicate any possible use of the dead children. Could it be a sex thing that some perverts needed them for? Or some dark, obscure group that required them for other obscene reasons?

Exhausted from his ranch work and from getting nowhere working on the murders and their motive by himself, Rico got on the phone and spoke with Myrtle Stockwood. She was the ex-hooker at Boise Control, his data-gathering group. "Myrtle, I've got a situation here I can't understand. I wonder if you could ask around and see if there's some perverse and ongoing use of dead babies in sexual or satanic rituals of any sort. Could you do that for me?"

"Mr. Morgan, I have already looked into it a bit and while I found some pseudo-sexual, so-called vampire groups that have sex with plenty of blood on hand, the blood comes from slaughter houses of one sort or another. Not human. They don't use babies for anything. However, I have a few untapped sources in Holland and England that might be of help. I'll check with them if you like."

"Yes, please. These babies are about five months along, if that matters. Thank you, dear."

Next Rico phoned another Control member in Boise, G. Willie Kers, who had spent a lifetime traveling the world for the Chrysler Corporation. "Willie, I'd like you to ask some of your friends in the Far East, as in mainland China and Japan, and also Germany, England, and maybe Italy, if they have encountered any possible use for, er, unborn babies at the approximate five-month stage. I'm looking for anomalies or off-center groups that might have some clandestine use for them, or for their body parts."

The retired Chrysler executive wheezed into the phone over his cigar. "Rico, I'll see what I can find out. I've heard of some strange items showing up on the grille at some barbeques in those countries, especially Korea and China. I mean they fry up dogs, cats, rats, parrots, you-name-it. They might go for roast leg of baby, too."

"Thank you. We're looking for anything unusual, in situations or in a person or people who might benefit from some extraction, or body parts, from unborn babies. Maybe zombies are eating their brains, or a group of loonies is feeding them to werewolves. Any sort of odd situation or people who pop up might give us a clue."

"They're too old for stem-cell work, then? And too young for organ implants. Looks like a tough row to hoe," returned Willie.

"Do your best, my friend." Rico hung up the phone.

Two days later Rico got a call from I. Yeats Prunzalot at Boise Control. "Mr. Morgan, through the kind efforts of Mr. Kers, Miss Stockwood and Miss DaKrotch we have found an anomaly in England." Yeats spoke with a slight accent. "Yes indeedy. Through a, er, slight intercept of British intelligence, combined with hearsay that Mr. Kers picked up which in turn gave insight to Miss Stockwood, we discovered the existence of a certain unusual man in England. Miss Tudarite was able to get verbal confirmation from one of the members of the Trump administration that this information is essentially correct. The evidence shows that this singular man has ties to several Members of Parliament who in turn have ties to our Senator Likkaman. This man is in his mid-seventies but he appears to be about thirty years old, and most definitely acts as though he were. A blue liquid was mentioned, but I regret to tell you there was some parts of the intelligence agenda that I could not discover with our digging operation. Further, good sir, it appears this individual has made some sort of contact with a certain violinist of your acquaintance. One more point in our investigation is that this man arrived in England directly from Germany, but the man in question is definitely Chinese."

"From where in Germany?"

"From Hamburg, in which city, curiously enough, there is a company called Chemische Vielfalt, which translates to Chemical Diversity. The company is a research facility, and in conjunction with China is working on some concepts of advanced stem-cell research. They are being tight-lipped about it, all top secret stuff."

112

"Yeats, that's interesting, but you don't actually know what the blue liquid is, or if it has anything to do with that German chemical concern?"

"It seems likely, but no, we have no proof."

"And we don't know if any baby parts are going to Germany, do we."

"No, we don't. That seems to be a dead end so far."

"Yes...especially for the kids, and for their mothers, too."

"All of us here in Boise think it might be a good idea for you to go to Germany to look into this," said Yeats.

"Thanks, Yeats. I gotta think this over."

Rico paced his rooms and then went outside in the chill late-winter air. "What the hell, Birdie." Rico sat on his front porch in the cold and talked with his beloved dog. This whole thing seems so outrageous it's like a dream. But no, there's a fresh bullet hole in this big Ponderosa next to us, my dear dog. Definitely not a dream."

"*Ruff!*" she replied.

The next day as Rico was about to go start up his tractor to again plow a fresh skiff of snow off his driveway the phone stopped him.

"Rico, it's Kikkan. I got something from one Roxy Roades you might want to check out. She contacted me, said she was a friend of yours, and had some information for you.

"She is. Go ahead."

"It seems there's an international group of U.S. Congressmen, members of British Parliament, and maybe a few from other countries here and there. They are secretly organized under a name that rang a bell with me. They're called loosely the "New Blue Antiquities." They're all old men and a few old women with lots of money. I haven't been able to find out much about what they do, but they're definitely a clandestine group. I asked Yeats to do a quick lookup and he found some redacted emails, but nothing clean nor clear. He told me to call you because Roxy found 'em and contacted me and I found a little bit more. But we really don't know much about 'em, so it might be a whole lotta crap."

"What actually do you and Roxy know about this group?"

"They are all old, yet active. We saw some references to golfers, yachtsmen, polo players, one who's a rock and mountain climber, and maybe some references to swimming or long-distance running. It's like they have a drive to stay active despite their advanced years."

"Hmmm. Are any of them named Rico Morgan?"

"C'mon, Rico. You're lots older than they are."

"Ouch!" He chuckled. "That's some well-done research, Kikkie. Any idea of a headquarters or any specific names?"

"No headquarters, and just three names. Hugh Grafter here in the U.S. and some guys in England named Dunwidth and Beagle."

"Beagle? Sir Phillip?"

"Yes."

There was a long pause. Kikkan asked, "Rico, are you still there?"

"Yes. Sorry about that. Kikkie, please send a telegram or secure note to Sally Foarth in England. You have her contact info. Tell her, er, 'The hunting dog may be dirty.' "

"Got it, Rico."

"Well, darlin', hang in there and let me know if you find *anything* else out about these old farts. It might be entirely innocent, too." He hung up.

Rico wondered out loud. "Hugh Grafter was in Montana with Lick-a-dick, or whatever that fruit's name is. Dunwidth...I don't know anything about him. Sally seems to trust Beagle.

Still, I don't like it. He might be involved. Who else is in this?" Rico asked Birdie. She looked at him with her tongue out and said, "Let's go out and play" by picking up her favorite ball, staring at Rico, and wagging her tail. With nothing else he could do right then, Rico took Birdie out and had a ball game that was a good workout for both of them.

Next morning it was G. Willie Kers on the phone to Rico Morgan. "Mr. Morgan, an unusual request came to me through an old political associate in Germany. I spoke with him while I was hunting down info on that chemical-research place. He's fairly high up in the Chancellery, and he told me he spoke with the head of research at the facility, a Dr. Grabnuts or something like that. Today a man from Chemische Vielfalt's main office invited you to Hamburg to tour the plant and talk with their chief. You'd probably be able to speak with his research team there at the company. The team here in Boise believes you could gain insight into this problem if you went to Germany.

"An invitation, eh? Crap. I suppose I'd better go. If I get lucky it might confirm that the German company is associated with the young-looking old boy in England. But if they're using dead babies in the mix I don't think they'd let us know. Er...Grabnuts?"

"Something like that."

Three days later Rico landed in Hamburg, Germany. He was out of his comfort zone and felt vulnerable. He was unarmed, and that was probably most of it, he told himself. Boise Control told Rico his contact at the German airport would be a woman who spoke excellent English, which reassured him because his high-school German was mostly gone, and what little remained sucked. He traveled light, no checked luggage. All he needed for a two- or three-day trip was in an old Samsonite briefcase that had seen better days. Walking off the disembarking area he was confronted by a big, strong-looking German woman.

"You are Rico Morgan, *nicht*? Come *mit* me, *bitte*." She mixed German and English fluently, thought Rico, and he could easily understand her, but was this the fluent-English speaker he'd been promised?

"And who are you to command me to follow?" He asked.

"My name Gerta *ist*. I have car." Gerta wore a dark red skirt, loose sweater, and black shoes with low heels. Her short dark-brown hair was combed back well out of her eyes, the sort of hairdo one might expect on Captain America, not on a German representative of a high-dollar chemical-research firm.

She led him to a five-year-old Mercedes sedan, opened the back door for him, and drove away from the airport. Rico did not know the area at all. The last time he was in Germany he was ten years old. Despite that, he realized the woman was taking them in a direction away from the heart of the city, and that was good. Rico tried to engage her in pleasantries, but she said almost nothing, concentrating on her somewhat clumsy manhandling of the car. She kept glancing at him in the rear-view mirror, as though sizing him up. Most of her brief phrases were not right and often made no sense.

Rico wondered if her English was any good at all "I'll give her a test," he thought. He spoke rapidly. "It was four years ago that the Chicago Cubs won the pennant in basketball when the trout were running at the steeplechase park, and Sebastian Vettel will win the world championship this year in go karts." He ended the nonsensical patter by stating, "Do you know a bomb was just dropped on Hamburg? How big are your tits?"

Gerta replied, "Yes, *ich denke das ist* ver' goot"

Rico had taken care to note the approximate direction of travel of the Mercedes, and now took even more care to pick out landmarks. "Where are you taking me?" he asked. Then, in German, "*Wo gehts wir?*"

"We to the factory *direkt gehen*. It *dafur* a few *kilometres ist*."

"Dis bitch cain't speak no English," thought Rico. "I smell a rat."

The city thinned, and Gerta pulled onto a narrow lane where there was no traffic and no visible pedestrians. A block down the narrow street they came to a traffic light and the car pulled to a stop. As soon as the car stopped rolling, Rico started rolling. With his briefcase in hand he banged open the door, hit the pavement and ran toward the rear of the car. A harsh "*Scheiße!*" and an instant later a muffled thud from behind him told him he had done the right thing at the right time, as a bullet from a silenced pistol zinged past his ear. He ducked behind a parked car as another bullet slammed into its fender and whined away down the deserted street.

Rico made for an alleyway on the side of the street between two buildings, which might be a dead end, he thought, as he put as much distance between raging Gerta and her red-hot pistol as he could. But no, it was a through alley. Could he get to the far end before she got to the entry? As he ran he put his briefcase over his shoulder to give some protection to his upper back. "I'm getting too old for this," he thought to himself.

"Now what the hell is that!?" Rico saw a car stop at the end of the alley toward which he was haring at his best speed. The driver was a girl, and she was looking his way.

Rico didn't stop running, and happily saw no active threat from the girl in front of him. As he drew near, she gave him the corniest, oldest come-on Rico had ever heard, which was as welcome right then to him as an all-Kevlar suit. She shouted at him in perfect English, "Get in if you want to live!"

Rico wrenched open the rear door of the car and flung himself onto the seat, slammed the door, and ducked below the windowsill as the car sped away. A loud bang against the car's rear fender told him the car was just in time to pull him out of the way of that last bullet from Gerta.

"That corny old line sure sounded good, my dear," said Rico as he sat up and ran a hand through his hair. He caught a look at the girl in profile, then looked at her face in the rear-view mirror. She appeared to be oriental, and as is the case with many oriental women her face gave no clue as to how old she was. She wore a dark blue coat over a light-blue blouse and black trousers. Her black hair was long and held in a ponytail.

"What would you have liked me to say? Maybe something like, Oh dear sire, wouldst thou mayhap enter my humble carriage to prevent your lame ass from gathering a bullet?"

"No, that's fine. What you said. It worked. Thank you. And who are you, exactly?"

"I was supposed to meet you at the airport, but I got delayed and you got waylaid by that bitch."

The girl, who looked to be Chinese if Rico had to guess, turned down an alley, crossed several more streets, came out onto a large city street, drove half a mile and finally ducked into a narrow drive next to an old brick building.

"Come with me," she said. Rico was not in a mood to argue, the girl having just saved him from a hot-lead proctology exam.

They entered a side door in the brick building and went immediately down a flight of stairs and along a long narrow passageway.

"What's your name?" he asked.

"I am Wun Fan Phuk," she said.

"I bet you are, but what's your name?"

"I just told you. We're going now to meet my brother, who has some information for you."

The passageway went on for maybe a hundred yards, turning here and there along the way. It was, Rico guessed, a remnant of the last World War, and had served some good — or bad — purpose during that conflict. They finally ascended a short flight of stairs and entered into what appeared to be the basement of a small house.

The girl led Rico up the basement steps into a small dimly lit room. A shaded table lamp sat on a solid old desk against the far wall. In a corner of the room sat a Chinese man of indeterminate age in a comfortable chair. He was dressed in contemporary western clothing, not the silk robes one might have expected. His hair was so blonde as to be nearly white, and he had a small pointed beard. He wore a blue work shirt and black jeans. He sat upright on the leather chair and puffed serenely on a cigarette. The smoke drifted upward toward a hanging colored lamp on the ceiling. A few cobwebs added to the decorations.

"Here is Wun Long Dong, my brother," said Wun Fan Phuk. "I must go now." She abruptly left the room.

"Mr. Morgan, I am pleased to meet you," said Long in perfect English.

"Likewise, I'm sure, but how do you and your sister know me, and...er, was your father a comedian? "

"My cousin Wu Long Wun, a fine fellow if ever there was one, mentioned you when I was in Kansas a few months ago. I was eager to meet you, but never like this. Wu Long Wun is acquainted with a man on your staff, one William Kers, and when you decided to come to Hamburg Mr. Kers contacted me directly to arrange for my sister to pick you up. But as you know, someone else got to you first."

Long continued. "My mother was a comedienne, an English woman. The English sense of humour is not quite what we have in China. Why do you ask?"

"No special reason. It's just...your names seem a bit odd, ya know."

"Mr. Morgan, do you know that 'Rico Morgan' sounds a lot like the words in one Chinese dialect that make up the term 'lame penguin'? There is no genuine humor to the sound of names from languages other than our own native tongue. I think you are somewhat misdirected concerning the oddness of our names. I think my wife, Wun Phat Phuk, would agree with me our names are not humourous.

Rico smiled faintly and asked, "But how did Fan manage to intercept me?"

"As I mentioned, Fan was going to be your welcoming driver, but someone else got to you first. My sister followed you from the airport. Fan told me all this on her cell phone while she was following you. She wasn't sure you'd get out of the car before your abductress killed you. Then she saw you get out and run toward an alley, so she drove to the next street and waited for you to get to her. By the way, how did you find out your driver was, er, bogus?"

"I was told the driver who would meet me knew perfect English, so I spoke fast American to her and she couldn't understand any of it. That was my first clue. I could tell she wasn't taking me in the right direction, because I know the research building I'm here to visit is on the north end of Hamburg, not on the southern fringes, and from the sun's shadows I knew we were heading south. Also, I saw the outline of a gun butt under her sweater when she picked me up. It all added up to bad news, so I bailed the first chance I got. Now, my friend, you seem to know one heckuva lot about what's going on here. Care to fill me in?"

Replied Wun, "I'd be happy to do so, but I suspect you want to get checked into a hotel after your long flight, and I'm guessing you're going to need a few items to replace your suitcase, which is still in that Mercedes. I can fill you in on the way to the hotel."

"A different hotel from the one where I have reservations would be just ginger peachy, but there's no lost suitcase. Everything I brought is in this briefcase."

As Wun drove Rico Morgan to a hotel close to the research facility in the north of Hamburg, he told part of the story. "Mr. Morgan, a long time ago my brother, Wun Thik Dik, and I got into a quarrel about the difference between right and wrong. It was some of the usual nonsense young people often discuss. I told him it was pointless to fight as we would both be dead from old age before we had all the fight out of us. He then said in jest that he was going to live forever. Shortly after our big fight we drifted apart. Then my brother turned to the dark side. He seemed to be going in what looked to me to be the wrong direction. He made friends that our late father would never have tolerated. Mobsters, they were. Then he went to the United States and got involved with some crooked politicians — if there even are any other kind. And after that he went to England, and it was some years before we heard of him again.

"He met, and cultivated friendships with, members of the British government. When we learned this, my sister and I hoped we might one day again be proud of him, but it was not to be. His friends included some suspected pedophiles and some of the utmost scum of British 'high' society. They were indeed high, on drugs of one sort or another. Accordingly my sister and I kept our distance from him.

"About two years ago we heard Thik was again in America, this time in league with high-ranking members of the U.S. Congress. One of them was a reportedly gay senator from one of your western states. That was the last we knew where he was until my cousin mentioned that you, Mr. Morgan, were thought to be looking into some sort of murder scheme in which my evil brother was suspected of being involved. I found out through my old associate Mr. Kers that you were coming to visit Hamburg, and was delighted at the chance to get involved."

An hour later Rico was settled into a different hotel from the one where he had reservations. Rico bought Wun Long Dong dinner. The two men chatted until late, and then Rico hit the hay and slept in peace.

The next day Rico made his way by taxi to the Chemische Vielfalt, Gmbh., laboratory. There, after some confusion with language, intent, and political persuasion, he was finally put in touch with one Dr. Fritz Gravenutz at the lab. Gravenutz, a slight man in his mid-50s with graying hair and slender of build, came out of his laboratory and advanced to the desk where Rico Morgan waited. He wore a long white lab coat covered with vague stains, and there was a slight odor like naphtha about his person.

"Mr., er, Morgan, I wonder what it is you are doing here." He spoke with a heavy accent. "I have no indication that I was to have a visitor today, much less one who expected a tour of my facility. Can you please explain?"

"Well, sir, I had an invitation to your facility from one Hans Fusz who apparently works here. I was told it is the express wish of your government man Willie Makit that I be given a tour of your facility, with emphasis on the operations of your own lab concerning advanced stem-cell research, all with your personal blessing. Are you telling me you know nothing about this?"

"That is correct, Mr. Morgan. No one named Hans Fusz works in this facility, and I know all of their names. Also, the representative of the German chancellery, Herr Makit, retired last year. There are only seven people associated with this company in my department, none of whom is the person you mentioned. I am sorry you came all the way here from Idaho for nothing."

"I see," said Rico. "Well, is there any way I can get some sort of tour, or information from you about your research, as long as I'm here?"

"There is a general tour, open to the public, and I'm sure I can get the personnel here to take you on that tour, but it does not include my own branch of the company. Our work, you see, is essentially top secret."

"I'll think about the general tour. Can you tell me, are you working with Chinese personnel? It came to my attention you are involved with them, as was reported in one of the science magazines recently."

"That is so, but again we can't tell you anything about that phase of our operation. The Chinese are providing us with some funding, and they also provide information on some test results they carry out in China with some of our, er, products, but that's all I can say about it. Now if you'll excuse me...."

Gravenutz turned on his heel and left the room.

Undaunted, Rico spoke to the receptionist and she agreed to give him the 'official tour' of the building the next day. "Where are you staying?" she asked.

"I have yet to get a hotel," Rico lied. He didn't like the situation at all and didn't trust anyone there enough to tell them where he was to spend the night.

The next day's tour did Rico exactly no good at all. He saw many of the operations of the facility, found it to be entirely professional, but never did he see any Chinese, nor gain access to the laboratory where the interesting stuff was ongoing. Unlike some spies in books and movies of note, he was unable to make a surreptitious getaway, grab the ID card of a lab employee, and explore the facility alone. He was entirely skunked.

The next morning Rico left Germany, almost entirely disappointed, but for one fact. He said it to himself the next morning in the mirror as he shaved, prior to his departure for the airport and home. "I never told Gravenutz I was from Idaho!"

CHAPTER 10
Leemy

When Rico got home from Germany he had a phone message from the local sheriff, Sam Fountain. Rico called his old friend. "Hi, Sheriff. Rico Morgan. What's up?"

Sheriff Fountain told him, "Rico, we found a man shot to death in his car two days after the shooting at your house. He'd been there a while, looks like. I suspect there may be a link between this dead man and the one I collected off your front porch. Do you think you could identify the second man you say was at your house that night?"

"Sure, Sam, I'll come to town and have a look at this guy and see if he's the same one. I'm pretty sure I could pick him out of a crowd."

"I'll save you a trip to town. I emailed you his photo just now. If you're near your computer, take a look."

Rico took a look and said, "Yep, that's the guy. I recognize a kind of squinty look, or maybe a mark on the side of his face. Might be a scar. I'm sure that's the guy who was here, never fired a shot, and then ran."

"Any idea who he was?"

"No. I've never seen him before, except for that night. I got a good look at him through the rifle scope, but I sure couldn't tell you who he was."

"You're right. That is indeed a scar. His name was Jake Auffe. He was ex-Army, good service record, honorable discharge a decade or so back, no criminal record. He'd been in town only a short time before you met him on your doorstep. Any idea what gives?"

"Sheriff, I wish I knew. I've been to New Mexico, old Mexico, and I just got back from Germany trying to figure out what gives, and I don't have the slightest clue. It's like I know something, when I really don't. Someone keeps trying to kill me, no matter where I turn up."

"Well, sir, you let me know as soon as you do figure something out. While you're at it, sometime you'll have to tell me why you were out in the yard with a sniper rifle on a cold night. Meantime, watch your back."

A day later Rico drove the thirty miles to town and went to see a fellow with whom he often played music. This fellow commonly hung out at one of the local coffee houses, or tea parlors, depending on your preference in hot drinks. The coffee house also sold baked goods, and was patronized by aging hippies, young single women, old married women, middle-aged townies when they got off work, and many folks who would be called street people in larger towns. Some of the local musicians played there for free coffee once in a while. The quality of music varied from god-awful to pretty good, depending on the mix of musicians of the moment. No one was playing when Rico walked in.

Rico got himself a peppermint tea, and as he paid for it he asked the young man behind the counter, "Billy, have you seen Leemy today?"

"Yeah, Rico. I saw him upstairs earlier. I think he's still there."

Rico climbed the stairs and thought about how he was going to go about asking Leemy what he wanted to know. Johann Leland Lhon, known as Leemy, had been born in Germany a decade or so after World War Two. He married a British girl in the late 1970's and they moved to Michigan, which had a sizeable German population. Leemy fit in well. He did general house-construction work and some finish carpentry. His wife collected dolls. When she died along with her daughter in childbirth in 1982, Leemy chucked everything, sold the doll collection for a bundle, came west, and stopped in Salmon, Idaho. He looked around, liked what he saw, and stayed.

He was one of Rico's better informants as to what went on in the town and the surrounding areas. Leemy Lhon, a distant relative of Formula One racing driver Kimi Räikkönen, knew what he was doing. He had his ear to the ground through his loose association with the local law-enforcement personnel. Most of his link to the law was obtained by playing golf with Sheriff Fountain on the tiny nine-hole course to the east of town. Leemy owned a pawn shop, but his assistant, Al Zeimers, another ex-patriate German, generally ran the pawn shop so Leemy could go off on errands or snooping missions and, most important, could also sit endlessly over a hot drink with his ear to the universe at the coffee house. His assistant did little of the buying and selling because Al Zeimers was a forgetful fellow. Leemy did the serious buying, and also did some jewelry making on the side. Between the pawn shop and his jewelry crafting he managed to make enough money to pay

Al's salary and to give himself time to hang out at the coffee shop and keep his ears and eyes open to the town's happenings.

Leemy's local knowledge had led him to many good bargains for his pawn shop over the years. He gathered inside information as he sat quietly in plain view of everyone, often with his nose in a book. To Leemy's secret joy, no one could figure out how he gained his in-depth wisdom and lore about the town and everyone in it. They didn't realize they told it all to him in their conversations with friends at that public watering trough. Yet no one realized what they were doing. It was like the in-depth personal knowledge so many people give out freely on their Twitter or Facebook accounts, yet Leemy's method didn't involve any electronics. It was simply sociable 'social media,' also known as overheard gossip.

People knew Leemy Lhon bought and sold things, and many of the locals went to him instead of to one of the auction houses to sell items that came from deceased family members. Leemy generally paid a better price than they would expect to receive at auction, especially for unusual items.

Leemy recently provided Rico's girlfriend Sally with one of her favorite violins, a Keith Hill that a local rancher sold to Leemy just before he died. Leemy played the violin and recognized the high quality of the Hill, but Leemy was an amateur. He knew the Hill would do better in a concert hall in the hands of a professional than in his old German mitts, scratching out double-stopped fiddle tunes with a bent left wrist. He knew Rico had a girlfriend who was a concert violinist and thought there was a good profit to be had there. Indeed there was when Leemy sold the Hill to Sally Foarth. Sally was delighted to get the fiddle, and paid much less than it would have cost her new. This gave her a top-quality backup to her loaner Guarneri del Gesu, and she thought the Hill might just project a bit better.

Rico found Leemy dressed in his standard uniform of gray overalls, blue work shirt and dusty cowboy boots, scratching notes in a spiral pad in the back of the upstairs portion of the coffeehouse. In that disguise and with his entirely plain middle-aged look and salt-and-pepper hair he blended perfectly into the atmosphere of the coffee house's upper deck, much like a piece of furniture in the room. Leemy looked up as Rico approached, and said, "Well, did she break the fiddle yet?"

"Not hardly," said Rico, pulling up a chair across the table from Leemy. "I think she likes it better than she likes me."

"I'll bet she does. That fiddle is a lot better looking anyway, and you don't sound much like a violin. So what brings you to town?"

"Groceries, mostly, and critter retrieval after a quick trip to your home country. I stopped by your shop and you weren't there, but Al told me you were coming here, and if I saw you I was to remind you about some auction coming up in Missoula in three days. Some guns, I think."

"Scheiße!" Leemy swore in his native German. "I forgot about that damned sale. And they say Al Zeimers is forgetful!"

Rico smiled. "Good luck at the auction. If there are any good English double rifles, be sure to buy 'em all for me and give me a good discount."

"No." Leemy smiled and took a swig of his coffee.

"Leemy, what do you know about anybody local who might have close ties to Washington, DC?"

"Ah, so you've come to me at last. I was wondering when you'd get 'round to it."

"What the hell, Leemy...!"

"*Ja*, Rico, I heard about the shooting, two guys involved, and now two down. I heard about the guy found dead in his car. Jake somebody. Doesn't take a genius to figure it out. Ex-military guy. New in town. Dead. One or two of us know about an attack on a private dwelling some miles outside of town. How many locals are gonna be targets for a friggin' hit, Rico? There's you, there's yourself, and one or two others who answer to your name. Who else could it be? Somebody selling bad cows to the Mafia? It's not like there's fifty murders a day here, ya know. Last one was what, five years ago? Ten? The guy you shot, Dick Gabler, was a loser from the day he set foot outa high school. Drugs, ugly women, a hot car or two, and a pea-size brain. Petty theft. His younger brother Freddie Gabler is pretty much an okay dude, honest, hard working. But not Dick. I'd bet good money he was shootin' his mouth off in a bar and got tagged for the job. I mean, Rico, who locally would hire a hit on, shall we say, a hard-working investigator? The backing had to come from out of town, and since you're in the business of helping foreign and domestic governments, it comes down to your asking me who the fuck I know locally who's a nephew to one of our senators."

"Wow, Leemy, you sure have a good imagination." Rico was staring at his tea as he said that, but as the word 'nephew' sunk into his consciousness his eyes flashed like two blue lasers at Leemy, who was taking a delicate bite out of a big cookie.

When Leemy said nothing, Rico went on, "I have a suspicion all this bullshit comes down to something nasty that has politicians behind it. I have a hunch, only a hunch, that I can name one of the bozos involved. A certain senator. But I can't see how he could want anything from me. I just don't know what's going on, so I'm scratching at any sort of clue I can find. Nephew?"

BORDER CAPER

Leemy sat quietly for several minutes as Rico sipped his tea. Finally Rico said, "Leemy, I strongly suspect you know something you'd like to tell me, but don't quite know how to do it."

"Rico, you ever hear of a guy named LeProsy?"

"No"

"You didn't hear this from me, Mr. Morgan, but you might want to check out Mr. Bugs LeProsy. His father was French, married the sister of a prominent senator in DC. I suggest you take a good, hard look at him, any way you can. And that's all I'm a-gonna tell you. Now, I gotta get going. Gotta plan for that gun sale."

"Don't forget the double rifles, my friend. English only!"

Leemy rose to leave. "Aargh! You and your exotic crap. If I buy any I promise to sell them to you for only twice what I paid for 'em." He left Rico smiling over his tea.

Rico chewed on this new information for a while as he sucked on his tea and idly examined the legs of a young girl who sat with friends in a distant corner of the loft. Finally he got up, went and bought groceries, picked up his cats and dog from his friend Andy the vet, and drove home.

"Woof!" Birdie bounced out of the car, scared the two cats, and bounded around her home yard, free at last from 'jail' where she was confined while Rico was gone. The two cats crowded into the kitchen and tried desperately to trip Rico as Birdie lapped up some fresh home-grown water. All three animals were overjoyed to be home, and the smell of fresh groceries promised a special treat for the three animals. They guessed Rico had something really good from town for them, and they were right.

After feeding his beloved pets Rico got on the computer and looked up everything he could find about Mr. LeProsy. There was not much. In desperation he looked up the bio of senator Likkaman, and after some serious digging he found out that Likkaman had a nephew by the name of Robert LeProsy, address unknown.

"Crap!, he said. "I give up."

Rico Morgan phoned his friend I. Yeats Prunzalot, the computer wizard of Rico's Boise Control operation.

"Yeats, Rico here. I trust you are well?"

"Oh dearie me, I knew in my heart it was you just when the phone rang. I was suspicious and now here you are. I am wondering what it is I can do for you, kind sir."

"What you can do is find out everything you can about one Robert 'Bugs' LeProsy." Rico spelled out the name. "He may be currently living somewhere in Idaho. It seems he is a relative of one Senator Larry Likkaman, also of Idaho."

"I am doing that now, Mr. Morgan." There was a slight pause. "I have the address, phone number, email address, work history, and marital status of one William Robert, or Billy Bob, LeProsy, also known as Bugs. He is single. What would you like me to do with all the information that I have now on my computer?"

"Jesus," Rico said to himself. "Why do I even bother touching a computer? I fumble all day and Yeats has it in ten seconds." Out loud he said, "Kind sir, if you could condense it and send it securely encrypted to my email address that would be just ducky."

"I am doing that right away sir, and I might mention there is a message from Miss Foarth here for you. I will send that along as well, encrypted as it came to me."

"Okay, thanks much, Yeats. How's your dad?"

"He is for the next fortnight with my mother in Bermuda, sick and tired of the cold at Yale. I think he grows old. I will tell him you asked about him."

Rico hung up, and in a short time he checked his inbox and found two notes from Yeats, one forwarded from Sally and one with the details of Bugs LeProsy, complete with age, height, local address, phone number, and living relatives. Indeed he was in Idaho. He lived just south of Salmon.

Rico was far more interested in what Sally had to say. He knew Sally had gone to the town of Much Dorking in England for one of her performances.

Her decrypted note read,

"Rico, I had an incident in the town where they apparently screw a lot, but of course they don't call it that in Old Blighty, so they don't recognize the hilarity of the name. I played Alma Deutscher's violin concerto and HUGE SURPRISE, Alma was in the audience and I met her and her dad. They invited me to their home between concerts. Incident: Post-concert in Screwtown with Gesu locked away with bloody butler to Ol' Whiskers, some "fan" approached me and tried to get me into his new Mercedes GT-S. He had a friend, both Mid-Eastern looking, who tried to help. I did not go with them, and Bruce Lee would have been proud of me. Just letting you know all's well. Next is Blowing Crap and thence home. This to avoid any scare you might receive via news of attack on fumbling U.S. violinist over here. Give Birdie my love. SF"

Rico interpreted her note that, after her concert at Much Dorking, Sally gave her priceless Guarneri violin to the butler of Sir Phillip Beagle (she referred to him as Ol' Whiskers only to Rico) who secured it safely in Sir Phillip's limousine. Rico knew the old man accompanied Sally while she toured in England, but didn't know the real reason nor the true association between the two. Sally had an English background, so Rico assumed Beagle was a distant relative.

With the violin safely stowed Sally had encountered a Mid-Eastern-looking goon who tried to get her into his car. He had a buddy, as Sally said, but both failed to reckon with her knowledge of self-defense tactics. Rico knew she knew some simple self-defense moves, but had no idea she was highly trained in Jeet Kune Do, so Rico could not know she had left the two goons bleeding and broken.

Her next venue was in Blaisting Fecus, which Sally and Rico always referred to as Blasting Feces, so the town became Blowing Crap in her message. The last bit of her note was to make sure Rico knew about the attack in case he happened to read or hear some news piece about a famous violinist getting attacked in England.

The really odd thing, as Rico saw it, was that the would-be abductors were driving a pretty fancy auto, one of the expensive Mercedes GT-S cars, the same as used in Formula One races as the safety car. How do goons manage to get a car costing nearly two-hundred grand? Rico smelled a British rat.

"Sally, what did they say to you?" Her old friend Sir Phillip Beagle asked her right after the attack outside the auditorium, his white sideburns, moustache and whiskers all shaking from his concerned trembling.

"They didn't say much, just 'Get een da car, beetch.' Luckily I had secured my violin with your man Jeeves, so I didn't have to worry about its being stolen, or damaged. I put a slight twist on one guy and slung him into the other, and when the first guy got up I gave him a lusty kick which put him down again. They roused themselves, jumped in the car and off they flew like a down full of thistles, or however that goes."

"It's 'like the down of a thistle,' and it's Graves, not Jeeves," said Sir Phillip. "You might want to remember his name if you desire to have him return your beloved violin. Have you ever seen them before?"

"No. They might have been Arabs, or Mid-Eastern, by their look. Israelis? I just don't know. But clearly they wanted an abduction, not the kicks and bruises they got. I nearly hurt my fiddling fingers. And where would I fit in that car? Does it even have a jump seat?"

"Well, my dear, I'm glad you're not hurt. Let us repair to the hotel and get you properly settled. Then I suggest you might partake of some decent Scotch to calm your nerves."

Later that night after Sir Phillip left her alone in her room Sally made a call to her home office in DC. Thanks to her training Sally had read and memorized the licence plate on the Mercedes and had written it in a tiny notebook in her handbag. She gave DC the plate number, and in a few minutes her call was returned. The car belonged to a leasing outfit that catered solely to Members of Parliament. That particular car was not signed out to any member in particular, so that became somewhat of a dead end. But Sally was now aware the abduction attempt had most likely come from somewhere high up in the British government.

She made another call to the Deutscher residence and confirmed she would be there during the week before her last concert in Blaisting Fecus. She wanted to brush up on some aspects of the violin concerto the brilliant young Alma had written and clarify every aspect of the piece before her last concert.

Sally went to bed wondering who she knew in the British government who might have given away some information about where she was going, and what she might know. Did it have anything to do with her old girlfriend Betsy from the 'States? Was it about the odd Chinese man she met a week or so ago? The blue serum she heard about from her old friend? What was it she was supposed to know? Why did they want to abduct her? Was she missing something? What did Sir Phillip know? Beagle...a small dog? No, that's not it, she mumbled to herself. She was on the brink of solving the entire mystery, putting it all together, needing just one more key, one more clue...when sleep overtook her. She dreamed about a small black-and-tan-and-white talking dog alternately playing violin and biting her on the leg, saying "Take that, beetch!"

CHAPTER 11
Backup

Sally Foarth drove north at the wheel of her rental car. It was her idea to split off from Sir Phillip to help throw off any pursuit by the Mid-Easterners who tried to nab her after her concert at Much Dorking. She had a hard time talking Sir Phillip into letting her go by herself. He liked to tag along on her concerts. But she was firm. "Sally," he said, "someone ought to go with you!"

"I agree, Sir Phillip. I'll see if I can get someone. But I think it's a good idea you don't come with me on this trip. I know you have work and it's a pain for you to go along, even if you don't admit it, and any abductors will be looking for your car, not my rental unit."

Beagle finally agreed to let her go without him, so Sally got a rental car and started on the way to her last concert. But she didn't go alone. Zak Dragon and Backup were with her.

Sally met Zak Dragon through Don Nikker, the noted British comedian and a friend of the Deutschers. Don was at the Deutschers' home when Sally was there on a visit during the week before her final concert. Sally was getting first-hand instruction from Alma Deutscher, who graciously helped Sally clarify some bits of Alma's violin concerto.

After her session with Alma, Sally met Don. "Mr. Nikker, I'm pleased to meet you. I've spent many a happy moment watching your performances.

"Miss Foarth, I'm a great fan of yours. I heard you were assaulted recently! It was in the news. Are you all right?" Nikker asked.

"Yes, I'm fine, though I believe the attackers are not so fine. I got in a few lucky licks and kicks, which drove 'em off." With a strong note of frustration she added, "I wish I could get a guard dog to travel with me. That way I wouldn't worry about being abducted between now and when I leave England."

"Well, maybe I can help you," returned Don Nikker. "I know a guy, another guy besides Guy Deutscher here sitting next to me. The other guy's name is Zak Dragon. Zak trains guard animals, and he's not that far from where we now sit. He may very well have a 'dragon' available that can accompany you!"

The next day Sally met Zak Dragon, chief trainer and CEO of Dragon's-Eye Guards. In his mid-thirties, Zak already had slightly graying hair. Sally thought he looked just marvelous, but didn't say so. She was also duly impressed by Zak's gift of empathy with the animals he trained. Sally made arrangements for Zak and Backup, one of his best guard animals, to travel with her. Zak and Backup would not only attend her final English concert, but would give Sally comfort and protection during the drive to Blaisting Fecus, and also during the remainder of her stay in England.

"Zak, I'm extremely pleased you can do this. I don't think we can get Backup into the actual concert, but I'll be happier knowing he's close."

"Sally, it's our honor and privilege to be there for you," said Zak Dragon. "I'm a great fan of classical violin and I hope to hear you play Bach's Chaconne, one of my favorites. I don't know if Backup will like it, but you never know."

"It's on my play list. I'll dedicate it to you and to Backup."

Even though the Blaisting Fecus concert was the last of Sally's current concert series, it was, Sally thought, a good idea to have an independent bodyguard in case the abductors got more serious. And so Zak and Backup were in the car with Sally as she drove a round-about route to the north-England town.

The night before her road trip Sally met with Beagle. "Sir Phillip, if I don't show up in Fecus by tomorrow night you can organize a search-and-rescue party along this route." She gave him a copy of her route, marked on a simple map.

"Sally, I don't like the idea of your traveling alone."

"I'm not alone. You remember the girl that was with that odd Chinese fellow, my old friend Betsy Jackery? She'll be traveling with me," Sally lied. The extra time it takes to drive my back-roads route will let us do some serious catching up.

The route, which she described in detail to Beagle, was not at all the logical way to get from Much Dorking to Blaisting Fecus. In fact it added some fifty miles to a straight-line journey of about a hundred miles, or one-fifty in all. That would add an hour or more to her travel time.

"Besides, Sir Phillip, I've alerted the press in Greater Biting, one of the towns along this route, that we'll stop for lunch there, so if anyone wants an autograph they can get it."

"All right, then, my dear. I'll see you at the concert in the evening at Blaisting Fecus."

Sally and Zak and Backup drove north after lunch on the narrow, winding road, seldom used since the Romans laid it down ages ago. Sally kept a weather eye on her rear-view mirror for following cars. She hoped the attack, if there was to be one, would come soon. She had no intention of letting the goons get away the next time they came for her. All went well until they rounded a blind corner and found a lorry blocking the road, and three men examining its rear tyre. "Well, here we go," said Sally to Zak Dragon as she pulled to a stop not far from the truck.

"I suggest we get out, leave Backup in the car, and see what the trouble is," replied Zak. "It could be a genuine problem with the lorry."

Sally and Zak walked over to the men near the truck. She noted there was nothing obviously wrong with the rear tyre. She smiled as she and Zak maneuvered themselves between the men and the truck, which put the three men's backs to Sally's rental car. The three men hadn't noticed the rear window of the rental car was wide open in the chilly weather.

"What seems to be the trouble," she asked.

The three men wore dirty work clothes, faded jeans and old coats. There were no markings on their jackets nor on the truck. Two of the men had beards. Sally recognized one of them as half of the pair that tried to abduct her after her last concert. She was gratified to see he had a huge bruise on his cheek where her high-velocity foot stopped, the last time she had seen him. He glared at her. Another of the men was clean shaven and seemed to be the one in charge of the three.

He spoke to Sally and Zak. "There's no trouble, miss, we just wanted you to stop. Very few people travel this road, we knew you were coming, and so we decided to get your autograph. The man laughed, and the other two joined in. The man produced a 9mm Glock and pointed it at her, and as the other two men reached for their own handguns Zak gave a sharp two-tone whistle.

Unseen by the thugs, a silent, black streak flew from the window of the rental car and in a fraction of a second crossed the few yards to the three men, all of them now holding guns on Zak and Sally. The first man, the clean-shaven one, had only time to shout "JEESUS!" which quickly became a scream of pain. In less than two seconds the black blur had the other two men screaming in pain and bleeding severely from the torn wrists behind what used to be their gun hands. The one whom Sally had bruised had his eyes wide open in terror. "AIIEEE! Allah save me!" he cried.

Zak gave a low whistle to Backup and said to the men, "Don't move! Don't even breathe deeply. Don't scream again or Backup will kill you."

The sleek black leopard crouched in front of the three thugs between them and Sally. His brilliant yellow eyes were fastened on the bleeding men, a fleck of someone's blood on his black snout. He snarled — a ripping, tearing sound — lips drawn back showing his gleaming teeth.

The clean-shaven man looked at his torn wrist, then at Backup again and said softly, "Jesus Christ!" and fainted. Backup started forward but a word from Zak stopped him.

Sally was grinning from ear to ear. She walked up to the bruised, bearded man who was clutching his bleeding wrist and staring wide-eyed at the beautiful black animal crouched near him. He stole a glance at Sally. She said, "Backup-U Akbar, shithead!" and kicked him briskly in the balls.

Backup gave Sally a toothy grin.

"Yep," Sally said, "this was definitely gonna be an abduction. Look at all this crap back here, Zak." The back of the truck contained ropes, chains, and a pile of rags. "Bastards were after me." Sally and Zak used the ropes and chains to secure the three goons inside the back of the truck. They bound the men's severely torn wrists with rags so they wouldn't bleed to death.

Zak searched them all thoroughly but found nothing. "No ID's at all, not a damn thing to tell us who they are." When he asked the goons, "Who sent you?" he got nothing but three stony stares.

Zak drove the truck to a wide spot on the road and parked. With Sally and Zak and Backup motoring on down the road again, Zak used his cell phone to alert the police that a broken-down van was spotted on the seldom-traveled road and needed help. "When the cops find 'em they'll have a good laugh when those goons tell 'em they were attacked by a leopard."

Sally laughed. "And then it's off to the loony bin with the bastards."

When Sally arrived at her concert engagement that evening she met Sir Phillip Beagle in the lobby. His eyes opened slightly wider when he saw it was she, which confirmed to Sally what she already knew. It was a 'tell' that he was surprised to see her, and of course guilty. Sally had *not* alerted the British media she was going to stop for lunch in Greater Biting. She shared her route only with Sir Phillip, so no one but Sir Phillip knew Sally was going to be on that road. Therefore Beagle either gave the order to apprehend her on that lonely road, or passed along the information to someone else that she'd be there.

Because of the abduction attempt foiled so neatly by Backup, Sally knew all she needed to know: Sir Phillip Roscoe Hornsbury Beagle, third Earl of Chutney, was dirty. She was not about to tell him she knew. That, she said to herself, is how good spies work. Before the concert engagement she had alerted her English NSA contact about Beagle and also her home office in Washington, DC. She told them she would not let Beagle know she knew he was rotten. "Not yet," she said. "It's a case of waiting and watching, maybe seeing who else is involved."

Her local chief asked if she wanted Beagle arrested to foil any more attempts of abduction. "Sally, we can just pick him up and make sure you're safe."

"No," she said, "I don't think it's necessary. This is my last concert and I'll be outa England in a day. That doesn't give Beagle enough time to do anything else to abduct me." Sally thought she knew why Beagle wanted to abduct her, but kept it to herself. If she disappeared and the news got out, Rico Morgan would immediately be on his way to England. If Beagle wanted that, it meant Beagle was connected to Rico's investigation of the dead Mexican women. "I don't think we have to tip our play to him or have him arrested. We might learn more if he runs free. As far as he knows I told lots of other people I'd be on that road. He's unaware he's the only one who knew."

"Okay," said her contact at NSA, not completely happy about it, "but if you happen to disappear we'll talk to him first."

Before the concert Sally introduced Zak Dragon to Sir Phillip, but did not introduced Sir Phillip to Backup. Sally thought it was a good idea to keep the existence of the leopard hidden from Ol' Whiskers, and she and Zak managed to do that. Sir Phillip asked about Betsy Jackery. Sally told him she had cancelled at the last minute. "I met Zak at the Deutschers, and when he told me he was a huge fan of classic violin I invited him. He made the drive with me, so I was never in any danger along that old road."

It was too soon for Beagle to have heard the details of the foiled abduction attempt. As Sally suspected, his main contact was the clean-shaven man of the three goons who got partially eaten by Backup, and that man was in no position or condition to make any phone calls — certainly not to a respected member of British Parliament. Sally figured it would be at least another day before Sir Phillip found out exactly what had happened. When he did, he would not believe the story of a trained leopard. "Big dog, it must have been." He told himself that until his dying day.

Sally wondered if Backup actually liked violin music, so she played for the big cat before her concert. If leopards can purr, that's what Backup did. Like an overgrown house cat he rubbed against Sally's leg as she played. Sally didn't want him to miss her concert, but he couldn't come in and sit next to Zak. Everyone in the audience but those two would leave, and that simply wouldn't do.

During the concert Backup was secured in Sally's rental car parked near the side door to the stage, within twenty yards of where Sally stood. She arranged to have a pair of small speakers rigged inside her rental car with Backup, turned to low volume. The stage technicians connected the speakers via a quickly set-up Wi-Fi link to the main microphone in the auditorium. This let Backup hear the concert as he lay on the back seat of the car. Sally and Zak managed to keep Beagle out of the loop when they ran the audio feed to the big cat.

The night of the concert Sally's heart was light. When she took the stage she smiled at Zak in the center of the front row. She knew Backup was close, and that was a comfort to her. Sally played brilliantly. Her presentation of Alma Deutscher's concerto was a smashing success with the crowd. Her solo performance of Bach's Chaconne, the concluding piece of the concert and dedicated to Zak and to Backup, was the best she'd ever played it. "Take that, Kogan," she said to herself when her final notes, the mournful double-string D, had died away. She got a standing ovation and had to take three bows. And that concluded her performance for the night, and concluded her concert tour of England.

After the concert Sally made her excuses early, and with Zak Dragon and his beloved black leopard Sally drove back to London. That night at her hotel room she got a cable from Rico's team member Kikkan DaKrotch. It read, 'R. says the hunting dog may be dirty.' So Rico found out somehow that Sir Phillip was not her friend. "How the hell did he learn that?"

She knew Rico Morgan had some slight connections with U.S. intelligence, specifically with Roxy Roades. "Could Roxy know anything about Sir Beagle?" She doubted it. Sally didn't know nor suspect that her report on Wing Hung Lo, the young-looking, blue-liquid Chinese man, had been accessed and analyzed by Rico's team, thanks to the skills of Rico's brilliant hacker, Yeats. She gave up wondering and packed her things for the flight the next day.

"One more night in this dreary, foggy country and then I'm home," she thought, just before sleep overcame her.

CHAPTER 12
Trap Set

Rico phoned Modesto on the secure line. "Mole, there's only one way I can think of to get close to the Arab goons who're killing the girls. That's to set up a trap with one of our own playing the part of a pregnant girl. And I think I know who we can get to play the part."

"Amigo, I bet a peso I can tell you who you're thinking of!"

"Yeah, Roxy the foxy. She's an agent and as we well know, knows how to deal with nasties.

"Dunno how much actual experience she has," said Mole, "but she sure knows how to handle a gun in a tight spot. Speaking of tight spots, have you got in her pants yet?"

"Screw you, Mole. In the first place a gentleman never tells, and...."

Mole interrupted. "When did you become a gentleman?"

"And if I did let on that something happened between Roxy and me you'd be sure to spill it to Sally in your graceful blundering manner."

Mole chuckled and replied, "Okay, so how do we get Foxy Roxy into the Mexican pipeline?"

"One of two ways. Either through our friend Eduardo Mendoza in Chihuahua, who could maybe get his Mexican Intelligence people to somehow infiltrate the crooked system, or...." Rico stopped talking and waited for Mole to catch up.

"Or someone else in Mexico who could get us into the border-crossing pipeline...Jesus!" Mole figured it out.

Rico said, "*Amigo*, I don't like it any more than you do. In fact it scares the shit outa me, but frankly I don't think Eddie's gonna go for it. It would involve his guys going deep into northern Mexico, and the Mexican government most likely will not sanction any involvement by their goons on the official payroll with the goons *not* on the official payroll who bring in more *dinero* to the Mexican government than any other source. So Eddie's going to say no, but I'll have to try him first."

All Mole could say was, "Jesus!" again.

Rico continued. "So if Roxy can do this I'll travel to Mexico and see what can be done from that end. I don't think I'll need you to go along."

"For that I thank you."

"If this operation gets greenlighted, I think you should go with Roxy into Mexico and continue across the border with her. I'll have to arrange it, and that ought not to be a problem because no young pregnant girl would cross entirely on her own. I think you could drive across from El Paso into Juarez, hook up with an informed member of the border-crossing guard, get to the border and cross together. That would give Roxy backup when she gets to the shack. Are you okay with that?"

"Of course. Well, it seems like you've given this lots of thought, Rico. The only trick seems like, how do we guarantee the baby-cutters will show up when Roxy and I get to the little shack. If you can guarantee that, then *bueno!* Sounds like the plan."

"Mole, you've hit the only thing I can't guarantee. We get the girl to the right degree of pregnancy and get the story out about her, a phony history of few or no relatives, bribe enough guys along the way to get her to the shack, but how do we make sure the Mid-Eastern butcher — or butchers — show up at the shack with sharp knives to cut the crap outa Roxy? Also, how do we figure out what they're gonna do with the baby once it's cut out? I haven't got any of that figured, but I've got some ideas. I'll know better once I get back from Mexico."

"Okay, then. Watch your ass in Chihuahua and especially points north of there."

Rico said, "North of my ass?"

Mole snorted and broke the connection.

"Roxy, this is Rico Morgan out in Idaho. I hope I'm not disturbing you."

"Hi, Rico. I'm just grabbing a cup of coffee in the cafeteria, so no disturbance. Whazzup?"

"I have an idea I'd like to run by you, but I'd like to discuss it on a secure phone. Can you call me at this number?" Rico gave it to her.

A few minutes later they were again talking, this time with the certain knowledge that no one was listening to their conversation.

Roxy, I came up with an idea that oughta let us nab the bastards who intercept and murder the girls crossing the border. Would you like to be part of this operation?"

"Maybe, if I can get it okayed with my office here. What d'ya have in mind?"

BORDER CAPER

"We send a ringer across the border, some girl who looks to be, and can be vetted to be, pregnant, and she'll also be the right number of months along in her pregnancy. But she won't be pregnant. She'll be carrying a gun in a pouch that makes her look appropriately in the family way. Do you get my drift?"

After a pause, Roxy said, "You want to get me pregnant."

"Well, since you put it that way, yes I do. And I'd prefer it if your offices didn't really know too much about it."

"How soon?"

"Soon's we can get you out here."

Two days later Roxy phoned Rico she was cleared to go. "Rico, I'm taking personal time off. They gave it to me willingly after that screw-up in Las Cruces. I still don't trust my own people over that deal."

'Roxy, that's great. We don't know who or how many are in on this."

Rico and Roxy and Mole set up a meeting date in El Paso, but Rico gave himself time to make a solo trip to old Mexico before his rendezvous with his friends.

He hated to go because he knew what would most likely transpire, but he had to at least try. On a fine cold late-winter day Rico dressed for Mexican weather with a dark, muted-check flannel shirt, his usual black trousers and light-weight shoes under a light winter coat. As always he traveled light. He caught a plane out of Missoula and swapped at Salt Lake City for a direct flight to Mexico City. From Mexico City he caught a short flight to Chihuahua and rented a car at the airport. He soon found himself knocking on Eduardo Mendoza's door and entering the padded room, but this time there was no playing music. There was only hard talk and hard consequences.

Half an hour after Rico entered Eddie's office Eduardo said to him, "No, Rico, we cannot help you. What you ask is nothing my men can do. They have no way to infiltrate the gangs that oversee the border crossings. *Siento mucho*, but that's it."

Rico walked out of the building, looked up and down the road, grimaced, spat into the dust with a curse, drove to his motel and made a few phone calls.

Early the next morning he got into his rental car and headed north yet again, following the road he and Modesto had driven some weeks before, up to the *hacienda* of *Don* Juan Cordota y Carazco, whom Mole said was the biggest of the big drug lords in all of Mexico. Now that Rico knew something about the man he was reluctant to visit him again, but it had to be done. Eduardo's hands were tied by government regulations and he could not help Rico, but Rico needed help.

Rico Morgan had a hunch before he left Idaho he would indeed be on this road going to that particular address, and now that it was the real thing he felt nauseated with an unnamed dread. It wasn't fear. It was a feeling he really ought not to be doing this, but after many hours' long thought in the company of his trusted dog Birdie, and listening to every recording by Christina Grimmie that he could find for solace and strength, courage and good cheer, he knew he had to go. And now here he was, driving up to the front door of a man with more innate power than most heads of most countries in all the world.

Shortly after Rico pulled into the winding drive leading to *Don* Juan's fortress, Rico found himself seated in front of the drug lord's big desk. Juan Cordota wore a gray sports jacket over black slacks. His light yellow shirt was open at the collar.

Cordota's black piercing eyes stared into Rico's soul. "*Señor* Morgan, what can I do for you?".

Rico lit the cigar the Mexican man offered him, but politely declined any sort of food or drink. The two men looked at each other through the slight blue haze of the cigar smoke. After a short minute, Rico smiled. He thought the best way to approach the subject was to be quick and blunt. Why waste anyone's time, he thought.

"*Señor* Cordota, I hate to trouble you but I have an operation coming up in conjunction with the Federal authorities in the United states to capture a pair of Middle-Eastern men, Arabs most likely, when they attempt to cut open yet another pregnant girl. I would like you to become involved, because the pregnant girl is not really pregnant, but is an operative of a branch of the U.S. government and will be part of our team. I believe our operation will not work properly without some significant assistance from you. Can I ask you for your help?"

"How can I help you, Mr. Morgan? What can I possibly do about those Arabs?"

"We have determined someone must alert these Arabs when an appropriate pregnant girl comes along. The target girl must be about five months along in her pregnancy, be entirely healthy, and must not be part of a large group. Preferably she will not have any major family connections left behind in Mexico. This makes her suitable for the extraction of her baby as soon as she gets across the border, with the least chance of heavy political repercussions."

At this point the Mexican man's eyes went to the portrait on the wall next to Rico. Rico had glanced at it when he came in and now gave it a long look. It was new. Rico suspected it was a portrait of Carlita Morales, the pretty maid who had her baby ripped from her dead womb in the New Mexican desert night.

"You notice the painting of Carlita, *mi criada*. I had the painting done in oil from a photograph taken shortly before she left for the United States." A far-away look came into Cordota's eye.

Rico felt sorry for the man but could say nothing. After a pause he continued explaining his plan. "I believe the alert to the Arabs who do the murdering and cutting logically must come from the last person to see the girls just before they cross the border, and that would most likely be the *coyote* who shows them where to go and how to get there. Anyone before that last *coyote* could not be sure a girl or group of girls were actually setting out to cross the border. Anyone else besides that last man could not be sure they wouldn't change their mind at the last minute, or maybe decide to cross a week later. So my group and I believe it must be the last man in the Mexican line, the last one the girls see before they cross the border, who makes the phone call to the Arabs. Once the crossing party is truly on its way and has indeed crossed the border he makes a call, the Arabs meet the girls at the shack, and that's it."

"You said this before, and of course it's obvious."

"I need to make absolutely certain the border-crossing *coyote* makes that phone call when my substitute girl crosses the border. We must be *sure* the Arabs show up. And there must be absolutely no chance of anyone alerting the *coyote* that the girl is a ringer and the whole thing is a setup. In short, no one must be suspicious of the girl, and the call *must* be made for that one specific crossing. We can't send dozens of fake girls across the border. We have only one shot at this.

After a pause Rico went on. "I know that you, *Señor* Cordota, could not possibly be expected to know anything about these border-crossing operations, which often involve the exportation of other, shall we say, somewhat questionable items, perhaps Cuban cigars, perhaps some odd vitamins, into the U.S., so it's not obvious to me or to my small group that you could actually bring any sort of control to this situation, but despite that I am forced to ask. I know you have influence in this area and I have been told your influence might extend all the way to the border. I have no other options. I emphasize again, if the last Mexican man at the border, the one who shows the girl the way, if he suspects it's a scam or a setup, then he would never make that phone call. He would know his life would be on the line because he would be jeopardizing the entire Arab operation. But of course we could be entirely wrong about how they alert the Arabs. They may use radio communication, shortwave or some other system, but a phone call seems the simplest way to alert the Arabs, and we believe it would also be the most reliable."

With a great effort and a heavy sigh *Don* Juan Cordota pulled his eyes and attention away from the portrait of the girl. "*Señor* Morgan, you bring the details of that fateful night into much too sharp a focus for this *hombre viejo*, this old man, again. But as much as it hurts me to re-live what happened that night, that pain also fans the flames of my indignation at the outrage performed by those accursed murderers. I would very much like to look into the eyes of the man or men who were responsible for that brutal act. And I appreciate your delicacy at not referring to the potential drug traffic that might occasionally pass across that border. Cuban cigars indeed!"

He sucked on his cigar a while, and then said, "Mr. Morgan, you are entirely correct. The last man at the border makes a phone call after the girl is on her way across the border. He calls a certain number and says a word, and that sets in motion the proceedings. I will not tell you how I know that, but it is so. No calls have been made since I found out that information. No more girls have been harmed. We have essentially stopped the butchery, but have not had, how-you-say, closure on it. When I say 'we' I mean my ranch hands and I, and some of the local police who know about it. As you know we are not that far from the border here, and I have a certain small amount of authority in the neighborhood of my little ranch. We like to keep things, *pues*, let's say *nice*.

"*Señor* Morgan, I happen to know the phone number of the party who receives the phone call in the U.S. but I could not see how to get my own people — the Mexican *federales* of course as well as my ranch hands — to act in your country."

Rico well knew the Mexican *federales* would have exactly nothing to do with *Don* Cordota's operation if they or the *Don* and his goons had anything to say about it. His drug operation continually filled his coffers and those of the *federales* as well, with continued payoffs to look the other way. Nothing but nothing must upset that cash cow, and the Mexican *feds* were not about to make noise at the border because of a few women killed in the United States.

Don Cordota went on. "Your coming here is indeed excellent. I will help you get custody of those Arabs if it is humanly possible. You say U.S. federal agents will be in on the act?

"Actually they are not yet aware of it," Rico said. "My so-called pregnant girl has connections to the U.S. feds, but we have not yet put them in the loop, so to speak. We had to set things up in Mexico first. We don't entirely trust the official U.S. federal-police people, for that matter. We would prefer to keep U.S. federal involvement non-existent for the time being. I have several men associated with law enforcement who can help me, though it would again not be entirely official. They would act under my direction, not that of official channels. I believe that would keep things under better control."

Because of Sally's obscure warning and Roxy's bogus trip to New Mexico, Rico was aware some U.S. politicians if not federal agents might well be involved. Rico planned to get help on the U.S. side only after the scenario was set up in Mexico. He didn't specifically tell *Don* Cordota, but he planned to do it all with the help of Roxy and Modesto and two other trusted men he knew he could call on, good people with ties to law enforcement. They were trustworthy, rough-work guys who were, like so many in Rico's sphere of influence, old friends.

"Tell me more about what you plan, *Señor* Morgan."

"I have a girl of the right age who's a trained federal agent. She's young enough to actually be carrying a child, and of course we'll arrange for her to look pregnant. She will come into Mexico with a trusted Mexican man of my acquaintance to smooth things over, and the two will go to the border town closest to the newest crossing point south of New Mexico, and then she will need to make contact with the first *coyote* to start her journey across the border."

"I can arrange that with no trouble."

"Then she needs to get taken to the crossing *coyote*, the last Mexican man to see her before she crosses, and then that man must somehow positively make the necessary phone call."

"Mr. Morgan, I guarantee that if you get this so-called pregnant girl to the correct location this side of the New Mexican crossing then the phone call *will* be made. All I need to know is the precise date this will happen."

"Excellent, *Señor* Cordota. I believe it will be quite soon. I'll be in contact with you by telephone or secure email, whichever you prefer, and will get you a photo of the girl if need be. Or we can use a code to indicate to you and your people she is the one for this operation, and the day it will take place. Or rather, the night."

"All you need to do is let me know — my telephone line is secure enough — and I'll make sure the path to the little shack in the New Mexican desert is clear for her and for your operation, with the phone call to the Arabs *guaranteed* to be made."

"Thank you, sir. I'm pleased you have taken such an interest in this operation. I understand that putting an end to this senseless butchery would make the border safer for your deliveries of, er, Cuban cigars.

"*Señor* Morgan, you are correct that I have somewhat of a personal interest in this problem, and about that I can tell you no more." Rico noticed Cordota's eyes again went to the oil painting.

I guess I don't need to know how you got that phone number, do I?"

"*¡No Señor!*"

CHAPTER 13
Motel

Rico flew back to El Paso early the next day and checked into the agreed-upon motel. He phoned Roxy and told her his room number.

"I'll be in this evening," she said. I'll check in with you when I get there."

"Mole won't be here until tomorrow morning," he told her. "He's got flooded in the desert, believe it or not."

"Not. I bet he's involved with some *señorita*, not with flood waters."

"Well, they do get flash flooding in the desert once in a while. Give 'im a break. If it's a lady, he probably needs it."

"What about Mr. Rico? Does he need it?"

"I'll never tell. See you when you get here, Roxy."

That evening after a light dinner Rico lay on his motel bed in El Paso, alternately thinking about his meeting with the drug lord and reading a good book by Edith Nesbit. The soft, warm smell of the desert came in through the screened window, and a gentle breeze stirred the curtains.

A soft knock came at the door. Rico peered out the window. It was Roxy.

"Come in," he said, opening the door. "Girl, you sure do look good!"

"Not so bad yourself, Mr. Rico Morgan." Roxy came in smiling. She wore denim shorts, a loose white blouse and tennis shoes with no socks. Her finely toned and tanned legs got Rico's attention. Her blonde wavy hair hung long and loose past her shoulders.

"Roxy, the game is on. I've made a connection in Mexico that will guarantee the phone call will be made so the Arabs will show up to gut you."

"Lovely," she replied. "Dare I ask how? I only just got here. How can you guarantee a contact with the bad guys?"

"I just got back from Mexico. I have a friend in clandestine operations in northern Mexico and he helped me set it up." Rico knew that was somewhat of a lie, but didn't want to let Roxy know he went to a genuine, vetted, bonafide, Mexican drug lord for help. He though it might not sit well with her, her being a federal agent and all. Besides, his Mexican-government contact, Eduardo, *had* actually helped him by refusing to help him, which drove Rico to the drug lord. Only the drug lord had control over the border crossings, and only the drug lord could have guaranteed the critical phone call would be made. It was a better deal in all ways, but Rico didn't want Roxy to know about it.

"So I'll go to Mexico with Modesto. Is he still with his lady, the floodin' flash?"

"Call him Mole. He'll be here tomorrow. He really did get delayed with a flash flood, of all things, threatening his place in the desert."

"So what do we need to do before we go to Mexico?

"Tomorrow when Mole arrives we three will rent an airplane and fly the border to scope out what my guys in Boise have vetted to be the new crossing, which you'll be using. We'll take vids and photos and scope out places where I and my guys can hide, basically do reconnaissance of the area. You can get some idea of the terrain you and Mole will be crossing. Might help, might not, but better to at least try."

"How did your guys in Boise find the crossing?"

"I have a genius guy I sometimes use, not part of the regular team. He's Byron Summers, an ex-aerospace worker I knew in Denver and Las Cruces long ago, back around the time I met Mole again. Byron's a whiz at reading radar and satellite images. My group sent him some data and Byron dug out the new crossing. I have no idea what he saw, but now we've got aerial photos of the general area, satellite surveillance images, and my guys at Boise Control overlaid these onto an aerial flight-software map. I'll use that from the airplane to pinpoint the new crossing area and give us all a look at the area, so we don't go in completely blind. We've established there have been some crossings there, but no murders, and also we haven't found any other crossing area for 100 miles that ends in a shack like this one does. The shack's well camouflaged, but my man spotted it from the satellite images. We'll give it one pass and that's it. No need to advertise we're up there."

"What do we look for?"

"See if we can spot the shack so we can get set up on it before you arrive across the border. The guy involved in a normal crossing sits in the shack and waits for the crossing people to come in. He gets a call during the day that a likely crossing's coming in, so he goes to the shack and waits, collects the drugs from the crossing party, takes the crossers to a good place to eat and sleep and helps 'em find work. We're pretty sure if a butchery candidate comes along the normal guy gets replaced by the Arabs, and they send him off, probably with a bundle of money. I'd guess the butchers don't touch the dope because that would piss off the Mexican drug source and also the gang members on this side of the border. As long as the dope goes to the proper U.S. recipient no one makes a stink about one or two girls gone missing."

"Dirty business."

"Yep."

After an awkward pause Roxy asked, "Anything else?"

"That's about it. Tomorrow we fly."

"Do you want to get back to your book?"

"No. I like your company."

"How much do you like it,' she smiled at him as she sat on the edge of the bed.

Rico's eyes drifted down to her legs and back up, lingered slightly on her chest, and then he smiled back at her. "I like it a lot."

She began to slowly unbutton her blouse.

"Can I help you with that?" Rico went to the bed and sat down next to Roxy. He could smell her perfume. He put his arm around her and put his hands on her breasts. Roxy wore no bra, and her breasts were firm and high. He toyed with her nipples through the cloth of her blouse, and then undid the remaining buttons. Neither one spoke. She moaned softly and put her head back on his shoulder. Her hand went to his trousers and she squeezed gently. He played with her naked breasts and brushed her neck with his lips and then his tongue. She undid his belt and unzipped his pants. She rose and tossed away her blouse and looked deep into his eyes. She sat on his lap facing him, her legs on the bed behind Rico. They kissed, tasting each other. Roxy unbuttoned his shirt as they sat together, and then she stood up and motioned for Rico to stand up too. She pulled his trousers down as he shucked his shirt. She had not yet exposed his manhood, though it threatened to burst the seams of his underwear. She rubbed her firm thigh against his bulging briefs. He undid her cutoffs and pulled them down, kissing the inside of her thigh. He planted one firm, adoring kiss on the center of her panties and then pulled them down, revealing the soft blonde hair, trimmed neatly in a heart pattern. Rico buried his head in her crotch, his tongue busy.

"You taste good," said Rico softly. "Lay back on the bed." He tasted her thoroughly, as deeply as he could. She moaned and groaned, grabbed his hair, pulled his face tight against her. She wrapped her toned legs around him and pulled his body closer. "I'm there! She moaned, and pulled his face in firmly to her moist crotch and came, gasping, shuddering, with soft sounds.

After a few minutes she pulled his head up, kissed him on the mouth, and said softly, "Your turn."

She put him on the bed on his back, pulled his shorts off and started working on his throbbing member. She put it into her mouth and slid her lips up and down, and soon Rico was thrusting his hips at her lovely face, going nearly full length into her mouth and throat. She took all he could give her. With a groan Rico exploded, filling her mouth to overflowing.

Much later they lay together naked on the bed and talked about the trap they were going to set at the border in a few days. Rico laid out the operation. "You'll go into Mexico with Mole, make the necessary connections, and come back across the border at night illegally, waltz through the wide-open desert and up to the shack we have yet to pinpoint. A few friends and I will be there to cover you and capture the guys at the shack when you get there."

As Rico talked Roxy saw signs of deep worry behind his reassuring words and asked about it. "Rico, what's fogging you up? You look like something's nagging at you. What gives, friend?"

"Well, things are indeed set up, but they could go horribly wrong. I don't like the idea of sending you and Mole in there essentially blind, hoping the right things happen. I don't have the kind of control I'd like to have. You two'll drive together to Juarez in Mexico, and then to a little town near there where you'll meet someone, and that person will deliver you both to the first coyote, explaining that you both want to cross to the U.S., but you'll have a severe throat infection that prevents you from speaking. The Mexis would pick out that you're American if you said as few as two words in Spanish. That's all supposed to be fixed, arranged, but you never know. Thing is, some of the people leading you to the border will be in the know, but I don't know who or how many, so it's best you keep quiet all along the way.

"The second guy you see is not supposed to have a problem with your nationality because he's being set up and sent in under secure authorization. This second guy will take you and Mole to the border-crossing area, and then there'll be yet another guy, and he'll be in the know, but again don't talk to him. He'll take your money, because that's how it works and we're putting on a show for everyone and anyone who might be watching. We don't want anyone to know it's all a setup. The fewer who know that, the better. The guy you just paid is gonna give you what'll look like a couple bags of cocaine and send you skipping across the border. That's the general setup. Everyone you meet in Mexico, even the first guy, is supposed to be under the control of one man, the guy I've contacted. They're supposed to do exactly what he tells them to do. That's what I've been promised, but I can't check it all. In fact I can't check any of it."

"So what's your problem with this?" Roxy sat up on the bed. "Looks to me like we run the crossing, we get to the shack, there's the Mid-East guys, we take 'em down, and that's it. Right?"

"That's what's supposed to happen. I just don't like this blind setup. As I said, there's lots that can go wrong, stuff and situations over which we don't have any control.

"So what happens to the Arabs or Iraqis or whatever they are that we catch there? Ideally, I mean."

"All we can do is put 'em in jail. Maybe we can force 'em to tell us what's going on, like where they send the babies and what-all else they remove from the women. No dead babies have turned up, so they're shipping 'em off somewhere. What we wanna know is who gets 'em. That's the big question. The least we get is these losers go to jail.

Roxy looked pensive. "Rico, a personal question?"

"Sure."

"How come there's no woman in your life? I'm an agent so I don't have much time to settle or even look around, but not you."

"Actually there is a woman in my life. I just never get to see her much."

"Why's that?"

"She's always traveling. She's a fairly well-known violinist and spends a lot of time on the road. You may have heard of her: Sally Foarth."

"Oh shit." Roxy spoke softly. "I know her. Why didn't you tell me?"

"Well, you never asked. How do you happen to know her?"

"I see her once in a while in DC. I think she stops there before she goes on concerts, because she's there several times a year. I got to know her about two years ago. She never mentioned you and you never mentioned her. Christ!" Roxy got up and started dressing.

"Where are you going?"

"Back to my room. This never happened. At least we can make it look like this never happened. Oh shit. I'd never have...if I knew you knew her. Crap!"

"Hey, it did happen, but I'll never mention it. Take it easy."

"Rico, I'll see you in the morning. And this never happened, okay?"

"It never happened, my friend."

CHAPTER 14
Capture

The sweet scent of sage soared on a slight breeze and brought the defining aroma of the deep desert to the sensitive nostrils of the man. Crouched under a yucca bush in the New Mexican night, his senses tuned to every nuance the night might bring him, Rico Morgan appreciated the special perfume of nature and smiled to himself. He liked the wild places. Not many were wilder than this one, especially in light of the planned night's activities.

Rico eased his cramped leg, moving it so as to not make a sound. The fabric of his trousers scraped delicately on a twig, making the softest unnatural noise. Ten feet to his left another man turned his head slowly at the sound, took in the source, smiled, and went back to staring at the tiny shack hidden a hundred yards away in the desert. Three men sat in the pitch-black New Mexican desert, all dressed in camouflage, all heavily armed. Kent Drakkala and Lou Garoo, two of Rico's trusted men-at-arms, were the springs in Rico's trap.

Lou and Kent came to the U.S. from Europe early in their lives, both attended the University of Michigan in Ann Arbor, and there met Rico Morgan. Lou and Kent had not known each other back then, but each knew Rico from the music gatherings. They were not musicians, but appreciated what Rico and Mole had been doing musically, tipped many a beer with them at the taverns, and sat and watched the girls go by as they partook of the fine minestrone outside of Dominick's.

Years later Lou and Kent moved to the western U.S., and they kept in touch with Rico. Rico well knew they were both tough men, thoroughly trained in hand-to-hand combat, Lou by the U.S. Marines and Kent by the Air Force. Rico had used their services in the past a time or two, usually separately, but this operation demanded both of them. As they waited in the dark desert Rico wished he had brought an army instead of just the two, or four counting Mole and Roxy, to this rendezvous.

Rico lifted the night-vision glass to his eye once again. He examined the shack and all the visible desert around it. He saw nothing new.

Myriad stars provided nearly all the light, weakly aided by a sliver of moon. The desert was dark and deathly silent save for the tiny, soft night sounds that gave the wild desert its soul. A mile away a coyote sounded a brief yodel. Was it natural? Could it be a signal?

Rico whispered to Kent Drakkala, "Ah, the children of the night."

In an equally muted whisper, Drakkala replied, "What music they make!"

All three men knew it was a natural sound. There was no reason for any signaling of that sort. All that was to happen this night had already been carefully set in motion. There would be no warnings nor any escape.

A small light in the shack glowed through a blue screen on its one visible window. The shack sat in a depression in the desert, a slight hill to the north of it, and a small grove of stunted trees and shrubs to the south on top of another rocky rise in the land. Invisible in the darkness was the clever paint job that permitted this eight-by-ten-foot rough building to blend into the terrain invisibly in the daylight. One would not find it unless one knew it was there.

The men waited.

An hour later, like the ghost of a long-ago forgotten tune, the hint of a sound broke the silence and came to the ears of the waiting men. It went quiet again and then came back, ever so slightly louder. It drew relentlessly nearer. Coming and going at first, the sound built in volume and presence, became steady, got increasingly louder. After many minutes the source became visible. It was an old Jeep, built by Toledo's craftsmen decades gone past, yet still sound and capable of easily traversing the rutted desert road that led to the shack. Fifty, perhaps sixty years old, the Jeep had been made well, and with care would last a hundred years more. It had no top nor doors. It ground past the hidden men, made its way toward the shack, stopped fifty yards from it, and became silent. Two men got out and slowly and carefully approached the shack.

Rico Morgan moved his cramped leg again, and whispered to Kent Drakkala at his left, "These are the ones we want. Let 'em get in and let the other guy get away. Then we wait some more." Kent nodded, turned and whispered something to Lou Garoo.

Within a few minutes the shack door opened and a heavy-set man came out, took a sip from a can of beer, walked a few dozen yards to his ancient pickup truck and drove quietly away in the direction from which the Jeep had come. Nothing stirred in the night. Again a coyote barked in the distance, this time a bit closer but still far off.

The men waited.

Rico saw it first. A tiny light shone in the desert maybe a mile to the south. It bobbed and weaved as it was carried along the trail leading from the Mexican border to the tiny shack. They were coming. It would happen soon, now. The distant light went off again.

The men waited.

"Damn," said Modesto Pincata Buena to his comely traveling companion. "I'm getting too old for this crap, *amiga*. How can you see so well in the dark?"

"Come on, Mole, the path is as clear as a city sidewalk. It's the only way to get through the desert without falling in a badger hole. Just look where there's nothing growing, up ahead, and that's where we have to go."

Modesto knew this, but liked to complain to the pretty girl. It was also a way to keep the mood somewhat lighthearted and their thoughts temporarily away from the coming task ahead. Neither knew what exactly would happen. The plan was to enter the shack, now visible as a small blue light penetrating the looming darkness about half a mile ahead of them, confront whoever was in there — hopefully two Arabs — and once they determined they were indeed the killers, take control of them as soon as Rico and his men showed themselves. They might not have much time, especially if the men at the shack decided to eliminate Mole immediately. Roxy was made up to darken her skin, but her Spanish sucked, as she and Mole both knew. If the Arabs spoke to them in what was supposed to be her native language, which they would surely do, they might be able to tell Roxy was not a Mexican as soon as she mumbled her first words. But being Arabs, their Spanish might be as bad as Roxy's, so that was on the good side. At any rate the man and the woman approaching the shack knew they might have to act quickly once they were inside the shack.

"*Pues*, there's the shack. Does it hold two Arabs, or one man who will take our phony cocaine and tell us where to go to find work?" Mole stopped, removed his hat, and scratched his scraggly beard stubble.

"I guess we're about to find out, my friend." Roxy removed her pistol, checked its chamber, and replaced it. "I wonder what they'll say about you."

They didn't know what the Arabs would do to a man accompanying a woman. Mole put his hat on and remarked, "They might try to kill me right away, but I doubt it. At the other crossing point the girls were killed some distance from the shack. Nobody's been killed here. This is all new. We'll just have to see, I guess. I don't like all these unknowns, *amiga*."

"I'm right there with ya, Mole." Roxy wore a loose dark-blue skirt over her bulge. It had 'pockets' on the sides which were just slits that let her gain access to the pouch that gave her belly the baby bulge. Inside it was a Smith & Wesson M&P in 40 S&W. In her thigh holster was her favorite Centennial Airweight. Her loose blouse concealed a Kevlar panel that gave some protection to her vitals.

Modesto was dressed like a poor Mexican farm hand, old trousers with holes at the knee, and a red plaid shirt with a poncho or blanket over his shoulders that concealed his 45 Colt auto and a brace of spare magazines. He too wore Kevlar in the form of his blanket, and he found it to be hot even in the cool night air. Or was he just sweating the upcoming conflict? He wondered to himself.

"*Amiga*, it's time to see if Rico is indeed here." Modesto pulled out his own flashlight with its blue lens and aimed it to the right of the shack, toward a thick stand of scrub that he guessed would hold the waiting men. Dot-dash-dot, dash-dash. Mole sent Rico Morgan's initials in Morse code. After a short wait and from a different clump of bushes he saw the tiny but fierce blue-light reply, dash-dash, dot-dash-dash-dot. That was Morse for MP, Mole's initials. All set. Time to walk confidently to the shack and knock on its door.

Inside the little shack the two Arabs sipped their beers and spoke softly in Arabic. "Achmed, I am looking forward to this task. My training as a doctor will serve me well tonight.'

"Habib, be sure to not cut the amygdala and the upper end of the umbilical of the unborn baby. That is the key to this operation, as our paymasters have repeatedly told me. These Chinese bastards don't like it if there's so much as a tiny cut on the baby. And that's about all you need to know. Just be quick so we can get the damned thing to Billy's Ice Hole in town within the hour, and then we can go drink as much beer as we want."

"How much longer do we have to wait?"

"They should be here soon. The call came almost an hour ago, and it won't take the girl much longer to get here. But here's the thing. The caller said 'one.' No woman crosses alone, so she will most likely have some man with her, a brother or cousin, maybe her husband or lover. We will take them to the west maybe 50 yards, maybe 100, and do the work there. We must not do anything here in the shack. The man? We'll eliminate him along with the girl when we get them away from here."

"Too bad for him."

BORDER CAPER

Out in the desert Rico glanced at Lou Garoo, who was pumping the air with his fist. Lou understood Arabic perfectly. Lou Garoo, like Kent Drakkala, was born in old Europe, in Czechoslovakia in contrast to Drakkala's Rumania. When Rico saw Lou's eager fist pumping, he knew Lou had recorded something good on the parabolic-mirror long-range auditory pickup. Everything the men in the cabin were saying was being recorded. Rico didn't have a lot of faith in the remote listener and had wanted to bug the cabin, but when they arrived on the scene it was already occupied by the normal watchman. So it had to be the magic ear, as Lou called it. Rico hoped Lou would get good evidence to nail the Arabs, and of course Lou got it. Lou whispered to Kent who passed it along to Rico: "They will take them away from the cabin to do the killing, so we can jump them when they come out." Rico nodded agreement.

Not long now.

Mole and Roxy were at the cabin door, and with a triple flash of his light, Mole told Rico they were about to go in. The Arabs heard the muffled knock on the door, and as it swung open Habib stayed in the shadows with a drawn but concealed gun. Achmed spoke to them in Spanish. "*Hola, amigos*. Welcome to the United States. This is my partner José," indicating Habib, "who doesn't have a voice. He cannot talk, and that's good for keeping secrets, no? What are your names?"

Mole spoke for both of them. "I am Juan Diaz and this is my cousin Rita. Rita has a sore throat so she can't talk either. Hey, *paisano*, you don't look much like a Mexican. Where you from? And do you have any more of that *cerveza*?" He indicated the beer.

"*¡Claro que sí!* Here's a beer for each of you." Mole opened a can and took a swig. Roxy took the can but left it unopened.

"Where do we go from here?" Mole asked.

So far Roxy had not said a word but for a creaky "*Hola*" when they first entered the shack. She kept the corner of her eye on Habib, who had come out of the corner after having cautiously put his gun away, but not so cautiously that Roxy had not seen it. She slipped her hands inside her tunic, through the slits, and placed one hand on her belly and the other on the butt of the concealed S&W M&P 40. Something about Habib bothered her.

"Well," replied Achmed to Mole's question, "we head about fifty yards to the west and there's a truck waiting to take you in to El Paso on a good road. Finish your beer and we'll get going. But first you should have a package for me, eh?"

"Ah, yes," spoke Mole, and from his shoulder bag brought out what looked like a kilo of cocaine in two packages. "This would be yours, I guess." He handed the packages of white powder in the plastic wraps to Achmed, who put them in a plastic bag and placed the bag on the table.

"Someone comes later to pick that up," he explained.

"Okay, kids," said Achmed, still speaking in Spanish, "let's head out." He took the lead out the door, followed by Roxy and Mole, and then Habib.

With all four people out the door, Achmed turned to the west and began to follow a path lightly defined in the desert brush. Achmed had not gone twenty feet when Rico, Kent and Lou stood up, Rico in front of Achmed, and Lou and Kent on either side of the column. Rico and his men had powerful flashlights and powerful weapons pointed at the group.

"Stop, and raise your hands." Rico spoke in a conversational tone in English, which he knew Achmed well understood. Achmed stopped, muttered a curse, and looked to his right and left. A glance behind him showed Mole's 45 pointed at his back.

He realized he was well covered and slowly raised his hands. At the rear of the column Habib, not as well covered, went for his gun, only to find Roxy had hers out first and had it pointed at his midsection. A typical Sharia Muslim, he had the extremely low esteem that sect has about women, and continued to dig for his gun. Roxy promptly shot him in the thigh, which dropped him to the ground screaming and stopped his foolishness long enough for her to retrieve his gun. She accidentally stepped on his shot leg as she did so, and accidentally twisted her foot over the wound, which got Habib's undivided attention, something no other woman had ever accomplished. He announced his surprise with a higher volume of screams

"Well," said Achmed, as Habib sat screaming on the ground, "what is the meaning of this? We were only going to take this man and woman to find a job in El Paso. Is this a robbery?"

"No, shithead, this is where your trail ends." Rico stepped closer to the Arab. "You are under arrest for the murders of at least two women and for plotting the deaths of this man and woman. That man there on your left with the subgun pointed at your balls knows your language and can play you a tape of your conversation with ol' Noisy on the ground back there. We know what you've been up to and what you were planning. As they say in the funny papers, the jig's up. It would be good if you told us the name of your contact at Billy's Ice Hole in El Paso. It might go better for you."

Achmed smiled and said, "As they say in the funny papers, go screw yourself. And you know damned well you citizens can't get legitimate evidence with unauthorized tapes. No way do you have anything on us."

"The girl who knows how to use that gun she has pointed at your buddy is CIA. My other friend here with the subgun pointed at your crotch," Rico indicated Lou Garoo, "happens to be a sheriff's deputy on loan for the occasion. The guy with the HK-91 there is in military intelligence, so you're out of luck, asshole."

"Oh yes, you Arab asshole, we also have you for attempted murder." This was Mole talking. "I recognize you from that attempted hit on the highway north of El Paso a month ago. Pity we didn't get both you and your lame friend. Tell Noisy back there, if you can get him to stop that howling, that you left his predecessor for coyote meat out in the desert. I'm sure he'd like to know that."

"Shit," said Achmed. "he was dead. What difference did it make?"

"Thanks for admitting you were there. We have five witnesses who just heard you confess to attempted murder, rectum. Rico, can I shoot him just a little?"

"No, Mole, we need him in one piece."

"And that, *Señor* Morgan, is how we want him too." The voice came out of the blackness of the desert.

Rico knew the voice. "Steady, guys, I suspect we're outgunned."

The four men and the girl kept their guns on Habib and Achmed, and scanned the darkness with their eyes. Slowly a man approached out of the black night. There were a great many others with him, some wearing night-vision goggles, all of them armed. They kept on the edge of the limits of vision of the group.

"*Sí, amigo*, you are indeed outgunned. I have twenty men here with me."

"*Buenas noches, Señor* Cordota. What would you like us to do?" Rico asked the drug lord politely.

"You can holster your pistols and place the HK-91 rifle and the MP-5 on the ground and step away from them. We do not want any trouble with you and your extremely competent companions. All we want is this Arab. I understand he was with another *hombre* when the two girls were butchered in the desert a short time ago. Is that correct, *Señor* Morgan?"

Rico holstered his sidearm and indicated to the others to do so. The two men laid their guns on the ground and backed away from them. A large group of heavily armed Mexican men surrounded the group, coming slowly out of the dark. They all had their rifles, handguns and subguns pointed at the ground, like the trained soldiers they were. A few trained their flashlights on the group.

Rico answered Cordota. "So far as we've been able to discover, he was indeed one of the two Arabs involved in that butchery, which is why we were taking him in. He was to stand trial for murder, and also, we hoped, answer some questions about who else was involved, higher up the chain."

"*Señor* Morgan, I give you my word anything this *pedazo de caca* knows about who else might be involved will be transmitted to you immediately. But first he has to stand trial in Mexico at a court more strict than yours."

"*Federales*?" Asked Mole.

"No, *Señor* Pincata. "*Él de mi.* My court."

"And what do you want to do with this other fellow. He's wounded." Rico indicated Habib, who had grown very quiet.

"You can have the honor of taking him in, and caring for his wound...as *ese chica bonita* did so nicely a short while ago." Cordota smiled pleasantly at Roxy. Roxy just stared at him. "As far as we are concerned in Mexico, he has done nothing for which we'd like to...try him, unlike this other *hombre*."

Four of the Mexican men came up and grabbed Achmed by the arms and started to pull him away.

"Wait!" said Achmed. "Who are you? What do you want with me?"

"Ah, *Señor* Arab. What is your name? Achmed, you say? *Bueno*. You might recall one of the girls you and your previous partner cut up a while ago was a *rubia*, a blonde, slim and trim with yellow hair. Her name was Carlita Morales. She was, you see, carrying my baby."

Roxy gave an audible gasp. Kent Drakkala looked at Achmed and smiled. Lou Garoo looked at Cordota and smiled. Achmed turned visibly white in the illumination from numerous flashlights.

"Morgan, you can't let him take me! Help!" Achmed kept up his begging as he was dragged away, pleading and cursing and trembling, all to no avail.

Don Cordota stepped up to Rico Morgan and handed him a box. "Thank you, *Señor* Morgan. You have no idea how happy I am that I helped you, and that in turn you helped me, even though you were not aware you were doing so. Oh yes, *perdóneme*, I must take the two "fake" packages of cocaine also." Cordota gave a word and a wave of his hand to one of his men who ducked into the shack and retrieved the drug bag. "You see, the drugs were indeed the real thing and we don't want to lose them. I regret any inconvenience I may have caused you and your excellent team. I assure you I will communicate to you whatever details I discover as to who else might be involved in this brutality as soon as I find out that information." He nodded to the four men and Roxy. "*Buenas noches amigos.*"

He and his men faded into the silent desert.

CHAPTER 15
LeProsy

Maybe a minute passed. Maybe ten. Rico wasn't sure. It might have been a century. He knew he and his team stood there silent and unmoving a long time in the dark, in the desert, as the sounds of the retreating team of heavily armed Mexican men diminished to nothing and they were left with the absolute silence of the night.

Achmed had stopped begging and complaining long before the last sound of the men faded. Habib too was deadly quiet, though he was wide awake. Finally Mole said, "Rico?"

Rico said nothing. After another minute Rico said to the wounded Arab, "Listen, Shit-fer-lips, whatever your name is, you are one incredibly lucky son of a bitch. He might have taken you too. Jesus! Let's get out of here."

Roxy and Lou and Kent didn't fully understand what had just gone down, but they supposed Achmed was in for a rough time. Roxy finally asked. "What the hell was that? Who was he? He sure as hell wasn't your buddy in law enforcement that you told me would be involved. How come I brought a kilo of genuine cocaine into the U.S.? How does he know you, Rico? Are you his "*amigo*"? And what the fuck did he just give you?"

"*Señor* Juan Cordota, biggest drug lord in Mexico, just gave me a box of Cuban cigars, Roxy. Cohibas, actually. Ask Mole to explain on the way outa here. Mole, you already knew Eddie could not, would not, give us help. I had no choice but to set this whole affair up through Cordota, but I didn't know, didn't guess, he'd be here himself. Please tell Roxy about him. But right now, Kent and I have to get this cooler to Billie's Ice Hole in El Paso, which Lou overheard these guys talking about before we moved in. We'll see who picks it up. Then I need you three to meet us on the outskirts of town, in that little breakfast place, the pancake parlor called Hanky Pankies on the road north. If we're not there in two hours come looking for our bodies at the freezer place. It's on West Seventh street where the old trolley tracks come through. But right now we've gotta see who comes for the ice chest and hopefully what he, or she, does with it. Trail the sumbitch and see where the box goes."

Lou Garoo walked off into the darkness with a flashlight and some minutes later returned with the rental van they had hidden, well camouflaged, in an arroyo a quarter mile from the shack.

Rico paused a moment, and added, "Achmed's in for it. That sorry bastard is about to get his share of hell over in Mexico before he slips into the next world. But understand this: With any kind of luck I'll get some good info on Achmed's setup and his involvement with...others. Come on, Kent." Rico walked to the old Jeep, made sure the ice chest was in it, and turned it around as Kent jumped into the second seat.

Suddenly Rico stopped the Jeep. "I just realized whoever is at the Ice Hole will be watching for one or another Arab to show up. I think we better borrow this guy, who says his name is Habib, despite his bum leg. Kent, you can hide in the back under that tarp there, and if things get rough you can jump up and run off all alone. Or help with the fight, as you see fit."

Roxy asked, "Rico can we do something to shut this guy up? Can I step on his leg again?"

They wrapped a piece of cloth around Habib's leg and it quit bleeding, but he started up again making lots of noise. Rico got his gun-fighting first-aid kit from the rental travel van and stuck the Arab with something to keep away infection and numb the pain. Rico always took the kit along on any serious mission, and used it on himself once. They roped the now-quiet Habib into the rear of the Jeep on a makeshift seat for the ride into El Paso.

As they approached the dim outskirts of the great west-Texas city in the late desert night, the neon sign of the cold-storage facility appeared: "Too Hot to Handle? Stick it in Billie's Ice Hole" A quarter mile from the cold-storage place they pulled over to change positions, hiding Kent under a tarp in the back of the Jeep and roping Habib securely to the passenger's seat. Rico threw a blanket around Habib's middle to hide the rope. "Kent, buddy, let's hope no one gets iced tonight." He got in the driver's seat and drove the last quarter mile to the icebox.

Bugs LeProsy lit a cigarette, glanced at his watch, and paced the shadows of Billie's Ice Hole, along the rows of rental storage lockers. He took a room in El Paso after his uncle Senator Likkaman told him to make himself scarce around Salmon.

In the past, whenever an attack on a pregnant girl took place near the border the chest or chests full of dead baby were delivered to a man in El Paso. He contacted LeProsy who would tell him where to send the chest, according to information received from his uncle, the senator. Bugs LeProsy figured, "As long as I'm in the area we can cut out the middleman and get the goods delivered faster. And we don't have to pay some goon to maybe screw up the job."

Twice before when he was visiting El Paso, which was often because he liked a certain local prostitute, LeProsy was the recipient of the ice chest. That was before the big media event of the remains of the two girls found in the desert by the pilot. Since then there had been no border murders.

LeProsy never liked to have to wait. He felt exposed. All he had to do was transfer the contents of the chest to an Air-Express refrigerated container and take it to the nearby Fed-Ex office for overnight shipment, but the exposure didn't please him, even though it was more efficient.

This night the new guy would be with Achmed. "What was his name?" LeProsy asked himself. He pulled a piece of paper out of his pocket and glanced at it. "Habib, that's it," he muttered. "I met that bastard once and didn't much like him." His inner soliloquy continued. "What the hell, why do I need to *like* blood-soaked butchers? Still, that Habib guy gave me the creeps. He's likely to do something wrong and screw up this whole operation. Why couldn't the Israelis come up with someone? No, Achmed and my stupid fag uncle Likkaman went on and on, raving about the new guy. 'This guy's great,' they said. Well, maybe he is. We'll see. But I still don't like him."

LeProsy glanced at his watch again, and scanned the road. "Ah," he said, "could this be the Jeep?" The Jeep came placidly down the road and pulled into the parking area. "Yes!" LeProsy stepped into the light and raised his hand. The Jeep stopped twenty yards away and the driver had his head down. LeProsy could see Habib, and Habib could see him, but something wasn't quite right. Then Habib broke the still of the late El Paso night.

"It's a trap! Look out! It's...*unhh!*."

"What the..." LeProsy reluctantly reached for his gun and watched as the driver quickly clipped Habib on the back of the head, knocking him senseless and cutting short his warning shout. "Who is that driver?" LeProsy ducked into the shadow and, looking hard, recognized Rico. With a curse LeProsy screamed, "Morgan!" and began firing at the driver as fast as he could work the trigger.

"Watch it, Kent!" Rico shouted just before LeProsy opened up. Rico took cover behind Habib, and as LeProsy fired wildly Rico could feel Habib's body shake from the impact of the bullets. Rico took careful aim over Habib's shoulder and cut loose with his 45 just as Kent joined in the battle from the rear of the Jeep. LeProsy had no cover and quickly went down under the onslaught of the two trained shooters. Suddenly the night was again quiet. The sound of death filled the air.

Rico got out, checked himself and found a slight bullet graze on his left arm just above the elbow. "Kent, check on Habib. I think he got hit."

Kent leaped out and looked at Habib, and said, "Yeah, he's bought it. Looks like he took about four in the chest and one in the face. You're lucky he was there, Morgan, and I'm lucky I wasn't sitting in his seat. If the fool'd kept quiet he and that guy might still be alive. Habib really fucked things for that other guy."

"Okay, here's what we'll do." Rico was putting a wad of paper towel on his bleeding arm. "We don't have jurisdiction here, so let's put Habib on the ground with the gun we took off him earlier, luckily a 45 like yours and mine, so the bullet holes in that guy will at least match the caliber of this guy's gun. The cops can figure out they shot each other for some good reason."

"Rico, this Arab fucker's gun is unfired."

"Crap. How about you take a few rounds outa the magazine, wrap the gun in the tarp and put a round up into the sky out toward the desert."

"How about I put a round in that bozo who tried to shoot us?"

"No, wrong angle, too much for forensics to dig around in. Pop one into the clouds, drop the gun near the Arab and let's get outa here." Rico started to walk to the dead man on the ground.

"How about I spill some whiskey on one or the other of 'em? Make it look like a drunken brawl." Kent held up a small flask.

"Excellent. Dope up Habib and leave him here on the ground, but not the other guy. I've gotta go check on him. I think I know who he is, er, was, but I need to find out for sure, and see if he's got any papers on him. Maybe we'll get lucky and find out what he was gonna do with our empty ice chest."

Each man did what he needed to do, and did it in a hurry.

"Whatcha got?" Kent asked.

"Not much, Kent. Let's get a cup of coffee and then we can go through what I took off this guy. Might be something."

They got back into the Jeep and drove off into the night, back the way they came. They were a mile away when they heard the sirens.

They drove the old Jeep north out of El Paso heading toward Las Cruces. Rico drove past Hanky Panky The All-Night Diner about half a mile north and parked the old Jeep in a convenient alley. The two men walked back to the diner where Roxy and Mole and Lou waited for them.

BORDER CAPER

Over hot java and scrambled eggs they looked at Rico's plunder. There was a cell phone, a small notebook and a scrap of yellow legal-tablet paper. After he ordered, Rico went to the bathroom, secured the door, and fixed one of his portable field bandages over the flesh wound LeProsy's bullet had cut into his upper arm. He didn't want to bleed onto the diner's tablecloth. Back in the corner booth the four men and the woman spoke quietly.

"So, who was this guy?" Kent Drakkala peered into his coffee cup to find the answer.

"He was Bugs LeProsy, the nephew of Senator Larry Likkaman, fag-about-town. The town is Washington, DC. It's one more bit of evidence the gay blade is up to his flabby jowls in this mess."

"But can you prove that, Rico?" Roxy wanted to know. "And who else does this implicate?"

"Entirely circumstantial stuff, Roxy. Zero evidence of his collusion. No I can't prove it, but in the back of the van, where I just now put it, is a Fed-Ex frozen-product container with a label on it, addressed for overnight delivery to Poughkeepsie, New York, to a fellow named George Whun. I found it next to LeProsy at the Ice Box. That's obviously a phony name because no one would want his name on a box with a dead baby inside. Now, when I was in Germany a Chinese man told me of a guy named Wun Thik Dik as being one of the worst he's heard of. His brother, actually. This Thik Dik has links to bad guys in DC, which probably means Likkaman and Grafter and one or two others. Let's assume for a minute that 'George Whun' is Wun Thik Dik. That means the babies are being shipped to him in Poughkeepsie. My guess is he's processing them, or having it done, and then shipping the extractions to Hamburg. We'll have to follow that up. Can you do that, Roxy?"

183

"I'll see what I can find out."

"Good." Rico continued. "This piece of yellow tablet paper has only two things on it, Habib's name and today's date. We can also check LeProsy's cell phone for phone numbers, speed-dial links and other stuff. I'll have my guys look into it."

Lou spoke up. "Why don't we get the hell out of this part of the world before we go digging into stuff and waiting for every local cop to find the Jeep outside and lock us all up?"

"Excellent idea," said Rico. The Jeep, however, is not exactly parked outside. We ditched it half a mile from here and wiped it clean. So let's get to El Paso, split up, and get together on the secure link in, say, three days? Good!"

They paid for the coffee and eggs, piled into the van and made haste back to El Paso, where Rico Morgan, Roxy Roades, Modesto Pincata Buena, Kent Drakkala and Lou Garoo all went their separate ways.

CHAPTER 16
Crossing

Rico sat in his twenty-by-thirty-foot great room with the music on, his chair turned to face the two DCM Time Window speakers his friend the acoustics guru Steve Eberbach had built so many years before. Rico still considered them to be the best speakers ever made, and he was by no means alone in his opinion. The music was Heifetz playing Bach's three Sonatas for Solo Violin, which Rico found better for quiet meditation than his treasury of the upbeat music of Christina Grimmie, the flamenco guitar of Mario Escudero, or any of the CDs by Grimes that he so loved. He first put Christina on the music system, but the slow measures of Bach permitted Rico to think deeply without the need to pay attention to the classic words of the brilliant late young musician.

It was two days since the night in the desert. Rico wanted a cigar. He thought about going outside with Birdie, his beloved dog, but she was asleep and Rico had a cat on his lap, his old bum Homer.

"Darned, cat," thought Rico. "Runs from my fiddle playing but sleeps when Heifetz plays. He also sleeps when my friend Jenny, 'The Hot Violinist,' plays her fiddle. Maybe I'm doing something wrong. I guess I need some of Jenny's lessons. I want a piece of cake. Why doesn't Birdie make me a cup of tea? Maybe I should've got married. Who would marry me? One of those young girls I know in town? We have nothing in common. Do you need something in common for married life? Just because I could be their grandfather, why should that stop 'em? Do I really want a wife? How about another dog? I could train the dog to make dinner. But heck, the dog would then *eat* the dinner. Should I buy a piano? Christina Grimmie had one. So what if I don't play. I want some Scotch. My house needs a new roof. My tractor needs a new tire. Maybe I should take a nap."

Those thoughts and a thousand similar ones raced through Rico's mind as he diligently avoided the serious brown study in which he needed to engage his brain, to figure out all the links to the baby-robbing problem in which he was so desperately immersed.

Finally he said, "Well, Homer, I better take a look at what we know and what we don't know." The cat purred, dug his claws into Rico's thigh, turned over and went back to sleep.

Rico's thoughts went back to Montana long before he first heard of the women butchered in the desert, to the night the politicians were talking, after Sally's concert in Missoula, about where to put the bodies. "That had to mean *new* bodies. One or two or half a dozen bodies at the border would be almost negligible with all the cross-border traffic and drug murders," Rico said to his sleepy cat, "but what if the intent is to greatly increase the incidence of baby retrieval? More murders, some in the desert, and at God knows where. That would create a stack of bodies to be hidden, so that jives with the DC buzzards' conversation. Where are the dead babies going? We know that some of them are being rushed to Poughkeepsie, and

Roxy might already have something on who receives 'em there. And no, boys, they're not being eaten by hungry cats." Rico's other cat Louie jumped up onto Rico's lap and sat on top of Homer. "Did someone mention hungry cats?" Rico asked Louie, who instantly began a loud purring. "You guys are two fat bums!"

Rico sent Bugs LeProsy's phone to I. Yeats Prunzalot for analysis, but Yeats found nothing but ordinary phone numbers of ordinary folk, though one of them was Senator Likkaman's private number. There were no memoranda or notes on the cell phone. If LeProsy had been in telephone contact with anyone in Poughkeepsie it had not been made with that cell phone. It was a dead end.

"So all we got from that dead dork was the address on the FedEx package." Rico swore softly to himself. "Come on, Roxy!"

The phone rang. Rico turned down Heifetz, gave his cats the chair and picked up his land line. "Hello."

"*Señor* Morgan, I have some information for you." The caller gave no name, but Rico recognized the voice as *Don* Cordota, the drug lord.

"Go ahead, *Señor*." Rico knew enough to not mention the man's name.

"I would have suggested you might find it helpful to look into one Bugs LeProsy, but I find out he's no longer among the living. However, his uncle, the prominent Idaho senator, is well worth a close examination — though you won't want to let him stand behind you. He might want you to bend over and tie your shoelaces. However, in your case you may find he would rather stick a knife into you instead of part of himself. Also a Senator Grafter bears close examination. You might recall I mentioned stem cells during one of your visits here?"

"*Claro que sí*," Rico replied in his best high-school Spanish.

"I suggest you look deeper into that. In fact I think you should look as deeply as you can look. Inquire about a curious Chinese man now in England named Wing Hung Lo. He is old but looks and acts young. You might learn of him from another Chinese currently in the Washington, DC, area, called Wun Thik Dik. There is also a German link that needs to be looked at. Be sure, be very sure, to examine the science of halting telomerase shortening, which Russian and Chinese scientists have recently and separately determined is enhanced by the use of stem cells and the spinal fluid and parts of the limbic system from somewhat older babies. *Adios.*" The connection was broken.

Rico paced the room a while, deep in thought. He recalled his own great interest, at his first meeting with Cordota, in what the drug lord had said regarding stem cells, but his interest had died to almost nothing when he discovered the most effective and most desirable stem cells were from early fetuses, not the five-month-along ones being taken from the wombs of their just-dead mothers. But now there's a new angle involving older fetuses. "What the hell is telomachoochoo shortening? Something like Crisco?"

Rico's trip to Germany to investigate a possible link to the young-looking Chinese older man named Wing resulted in nothing more than his getting shot at. When Rico met briefly in Germany with Wun Long Dong in his cloistered room, the man named his brother, Wun Thik Dik, as a reprehensible guy with contacts in DC. Now Thik Dik popped up again. "So, I'm supposed to look seriously into stem cells, spinal taps, and telapeepee shortening. What the hell is that?"

Within an hour Rico, thanks to his Boise team, understood that halting the shortening of telomeres, which form the end caps of chromosomes, tends to halt aging. "But can it turn back time?" Rico wondered.

Rico spoke out loud to his sleepy feline audience. "Could the blue liquid mentioned in connection with the youthful-looking man be some sort of serum produced from dead babies? And it makes him look younger? That's crazy. Yeats told me he suspected the blue goo most likely came from Germany. This is more confirmation of that, or so says Cordota. He suggests these older unborn babies may have some magic juice that prevents telomere shortening, thereby halting aging. What else can it do?

"So, is that why that bitch tried to kill me in Germany? Were the German experiments indeed producing something they didn't want me to know about, and was I getting too close? And what about England? Why was Sally attacked?"

The phone interrupted Rico's thoughts. It was Kikkan DaKrotch. "Rico, we found out the Chinese guy in England who is old but appears to be young takes some sort of blue liquid by injection, every other day. He's dating a friend of Sally Foarth's named Betsy Jackery."

"His name is Wing Hung Lo."

"Yes! How'd you know that?"

"Tell ya later. Anything else?"

"Yes. I found out that there's a tie between Sir Phillip Beagle and a Chinese man in the U.S. named...uh . . ."

"Wun Thik Dik?" Rico interrupted Kikkan.

"Yep, that's him. Wun hangs out in the Poughkeepsie area and apparently also knows your Senator Likkadick."

"It's Likkaman. And he's not my senator. I never voted for the bastard. Kikkie, that's more evidence Sir Phillip is dirty, or at the least, not the good father figure Sally thinks he is."

"Er...*What*?" Kikkan didn't know about the link between Beagle and Sally.

"Kikkan, forgive me. I should have told you that Sally has Beagle for a friend in England whenever she goes to Old Blighty. They have some common link to her former violin tutor over there."

"Does that mean Sally's in danger?"

"Probably. Anything else?"

"Yes. This guy Wun Thik Dik took off for London this morning.

"Shit! Kikkie, send a cable right now to Sally, care of her hotel. Keep it simple. Say something like, 'The hunting dog may bite you.' And then book me on the next flight you can get for me, Missoula to Heathrow."

"Hold it." A few seconds later she said, "Rico, looks like the next flight linking to Heathrow leaves Missoula this evening at 10 p.m. Can you make it?"

"Book me!"

That afternoon Rico called his neighbor to take care of Birdie and the cats for a few days. He made a few other phone calls and then threw a few things into a small carry-on bag. After an early dinner he hit the road to Missoula in his immaculate '94 Dodge Stealth R/T twin-turbo V-6. He hit the highway running and made the 120 miles to Missoula airport with plenty of time to spare. He would catch a link in Chicago and then sleep on the airplane. His flight would arrive in London at Heathrow around 6 p.m. local time the next day.

Rico knew that because his team had stopped the scheduled shipment of Roxy's 'baby' from New Mexico to the east coast the recipient, Wun Thik Dik, must have got suspicious. Wun would have tried to contact LeProsy. Most likely he talked to the cops or an associate and learned that LeProsy was dead.

BORDER CAPER

With Wun running to England Rico guessed that Beagle would make a last-ditch effort to capture Sally in order to get Rico to England. If he got there and Sally was on her way home, Rico would just turn around and do the same thing himself. But he didn't want to lose any time if she had been nabbed. The smart thing was to get to Heathrow ASAP.

As the next day waned, Sally found herself on the way to Heathrow airport, having just said goodbye to Backup and his good-looking handler, Zak Dragon. Relaxing in a cab with her small suitcase and cased violin she considered the message Rico had sent her a few hours before. So Rico had found out the same thing Sally knew, that Beagle was on the wrong side of the aisle. She pondered this as the cab slogged through the cold, foggy London streets toward Heathrow, keeping to the wrong side of the street as far as Roxy was concerned. "I'd hate to drive here in town," she said to herself. "It's okay if there's traffic, but if I found myself alone I'd drive on the right side of the street and bang into someone."

The cab let her off in front of the terminal and Sally grabbed her violin case in one hand and her small Samsonite in the other and started toward the building. A porter approached her and offered to carry her suitcase, but Sally refused. The porter stood in front of her and, carefully concealing it from the other people at hand, showed Sally a small handgun fitted with a fat silencer and said, "Come with me." Sally had both hands full, and didn't want to endanger herself or her valuable violin. She knew she could disarm the man easily enough, so she decided to play along and see what he wanted. Away from the crowd she could act more easily, too. She didn't want to get shot, and the silencer was an indication that that could easily happen.

He led her down a hall, up and down some steps, and then opened a door to another hall, down which they walked a good fifty yards, and then through a door. The room they entered appeared to be some sort of long-term storage area, with big doors that were slightly open. Everything was painted dull gray. There were two small, dirty windows, an old metal desk, a filing cabinet, and not much else. Glancing through the gap in the doors Sally could see they gave out onto what appeared to be the tarmac, essentially the level of the main runways. She could see a few people, apparently airport workmen, one of them pulling by hand a big box on wheels, another heading toward one of the big fueling trucks, another driving a train of baggage toward a waiting jetliner. "Not much help there," she thought.

The man with the gun pulled out a phone. He spoke to Sally.

"Sit there!" He indicated a chair behind an old desk in the room.

She sat. She decided against trying to disarm the man. She wanted more information and she thought the best way to get it was to play along.

The gunman spoke briefly into the phone.

"She's here!"

He broke the connection and pocketed the phone.

They didn't have long to wait until Sir Phillip Beagle walked into the room with a Chinese man in tow.

Rico's flight touched down at about the same time Sally was being abducted. As he got off the airplane and went through the passenger area he was accosted by an athletic-looking man in his mid-30s he'd never seen before. "Mr. Morgan? My name is Zak Dragon. I got a call from a good friend who told me you were coming on this flight and I should watch out for you. I got another phone call from someone who sent me your photo."

On the alert, Rico began to decide where to punch him to do the most damage quickest, but then recalled something he'd seen on the Internet a few months back. "Dragon! You're the guy who trains guard dogs, or something like that!"

"Er...yes, something like that. I've been guarding Sally Foarth during her last few days in England, and just today said goodbye to her. When I heard you were coming I smelled a rat and decided to make sure Sally got checked in for her flight home. She did not, so I went looking for her."

"Guarding her? She never mentioned anything...."

"It came up suddenly, right after the first abduction attempt on her, which you may have read about. She was visiting a friend of mine and decided to contact me to, er, back her up, for the remainder of her stay. We had one incident, so it was a good thing she did."

"The hell! Why didn't she tell me? So she's okay?"

"She was, until she got here to Heathrow. I'd asked her if I could come along, but she assured me she could take care of herself and her precious fiddle without my Backup."

"Do you know if she arrived at the airport? Or did she go missing along the way from her hotel?"

"I got lucky. A friend of mine who's a fan of hers ran into me here at the airport a few minutes ago. He said he saw her get out of a cab in front of this terminal. A few other people recognized her, he said, but no one bothered her, so far as he knew. He saw her go off with a porter down the hall.

"Well, that narrows things down a bit. If....Wait a minute. You said a good friend let you know I was coming? Who was he and how the hell did he know I was on my way here?"

"My friend, the father of a famous young musical composer, got a phone call from his old friend Prunzalot, who apparently works for you. He said Prunzy called to find out the current location of Miss Foarth and then told my friend you were enroute, and my friend informed him she was either with me or perhaps alone, and most likely on her way to the airport. My friend then called me, as did someone named Crotch shortly afterwards.

"DaKrotch. She's Dutch."

"She sent me a photo of you. I got worried, and here we are. Can I ask, Mr. Morgan, why you came?"

"I found out a guy she's trusted a long time and apparently travels with, during her concert tours in England, is apparently in on a scheme that involves murder."

"Sir Phillip Roscoe Hornsbury Beagle, third Earl of Chutney."

"Yes, dammit, that's him. A crooked associate of his just fled the U.S. on his way here. I figured they'd nab Sally to get me over here, so I jumped the gun on 'em. So you know about Beagle? Does everyone except me know what's going on?"

"I haven't a clue what's going on, Morgan."

"How about we go looking for Sally?"

"Good idea.... Wait! That's him!"

"That's whom?"

"Him! Sir Doggy! Crikey, he knows me. Can't let him see me. Look over my shoulder toward the main entranceway. See that guy with white hair and a big moustache in the tweed topcoat, with a Chinese-looking man at his side?"

Rico found him, and said, "You mean with the Chinese man in the dark-green overcoat with fur on the collar?"

"Yeah, that's him. He's gotta be here because of her."

"Or he may be just catching a flight. Let's see where he goes." Rico sauntered their way, keeping Zak partially concealed behind him, staying twenty yards away and hidden among the crowd of passengers from the white-haired, distinguished-looking man and the younger Chinese fellow. Rico knew he'd seen the Chinese man before, and quickly made the connection. He'd been with Likkaman at that long-ago concert in Missoula, when Rico heard them talking about the potties that turned into bodies.

Beagle didn't go to the check-in counter. He and the Chinese man headed down a long corridor leading away from the activity center of the terminal. Rico and Zak held back. "Morgan, that way leads to the baggage area, weaves around and eventually gives onto the tarmac. You follow him and I'll go around to the outside. I have to get something. I'll meet you on the field. I'll have a box on wheels with me. When you see me, wave so I can find you."

"Zak, wait a minute." Rico opened his briefcase and took out something and handed it to Zak. "Take this. It's a com device that fits in your ear and on your collar. You'll be able to hear me and talk with me from wherever you are on the airport. That's a better link than waving my arms."

Zak Dragon went out the nearest side door and disappeared. Rico Morgan followed the odd pair at a distance. When they turned into a distant door Rico ran to it and cautiously opened it, and followed them down a staircase, up another, through a few more doors and down a long corridor until they entered a room near its end. As they opened the door, Rico vaguely heard a woman's voice that could only have been Sally's saying, "Sir Phillip, I presume."

"Sally, I'm so sorry to have to detain you in this brutal fashion. You see, we need to get a friend of yours to come over here before you leave, and the best way to do that is to capture you and have him come to your rescue. I promise you we will not retain you a minute longer than it takes for him to arrive in England. I am speaking of course of your friend Ricardo Morgan." Sir Phillip Beagle smiled at Sally, which Sally thought looked more like a smirk.

"Sir Phillip, you have no right to detain me. What the hell are you up to? And what do you want with Rico?" Sally thought it best to keep her cards in her hand and not let the old man know she knew he was involved in the abduction attempt on the road a few days earlier.

"Your friend Morgan is putting his nose in matters of international security and we need to stop him. He has violated several laws in Germany and in the United States, and has acted against our people, and this must be halted."

"I think you must be mistaken, Phillip." She dropped 'Sir.' Sally knew he didn't deserve it. "Rico Morgan does not violate international laws. I believe you're making this up."

"Believe what you want, my dear. Be that as it may, you're going to be detained for a while here in England. I promise you won't be hurt. Now as soon as my colleague shows up we can proceed to your new temporary quarters."

The man Sally saw on the tarmac pulling a box on wheels stopped, pressed his hand against his ear, and spoke into his collar. "Morgan, any sign of 'em?"

"Zak, I've traced 'em to a room that apparently gives out onto the tarmac. I'm in the room next to it, and I can see you through this dingy window. Keep coming the way you are for another fifty yards and you'll be here."

Zak left the box on wheels outside Rico's room on the edge of the tarmac.

"What the hell's in that box?"

"A friend of Sally's," replied Zak. "One of my guard animals."

"Like a dog?"

"Sort of like a dog, yes."

"The Beagle and his Chink are in the next room with Sally. I heard Beagle telling Sally she's going to be held here until I show up. He's in for a rude surprise. Let's see what else we can hear."

Just then the door to the hall opened and a man walked in on Rico and Zak. He looked youngish, definitely Chinese, athletic, and highly imposing because of the gun he had trained on Rico and Zak. "Gentlemen! I think you can find out what's going on in the next room most easily by coming with me."

"Who in blazes are you?" asked Rico.

"Mr. Morgan, you can call me Wing," said Wing Hung Lo.

"How'd you know my name?"

"I was given some photos of you by a friend in the U.S. He thought you might be coming this way soon, but you got here before you were expected. Luckily I recognized you in the lobby on my way to meet a friend, and followed you down here." Wing grinned.

Rico could tell Wing was no gunman by the way he held his 9mm SIG, but he thought Wing would let him and Zak make an easy entrance into the next room, and then they could find out more about what was going on before taking action.

The sun was just setting as Rico and Zak walked into the next room in front of Wing's gun.

CHAPTER 17
Explanations

When Rico and Zak walked into the room where Sally, Wun Thik Dik and Sir Phillip Beagle were, Sally gave little indication of surprise.

Wing said, "Sir Phillip, I present you Ricardo Morgan."

Beagle's eyes opened wide and he gave a big grin.

"Just the man I wanted to see!" burst out the old whiskered gentleman. "Mr. Morgan, what a delightful surprise. I thought I'd have to wait at least a few days, until you found out about Sally here. Welcome! Welcome to London!"

"Nice to know I'm a few days ahead of your schedule, you crooked old fart. What the hell do you think you're doing, and why do you think I have anything you want?"

"Mr. Morgan, I had every intention of letting young Sally here go when you arrived, but now it seems you have bungled up her impending freedom by arriving too soon."

"Bullshit, you old fool. Do you think Sally or I are so stupid to think you could have let her go when you already have her at gunpoint?" Rico was not at all happy that Sir Phillip tried to make Rico the cause of Sally's fate. "Cut the crap and tell me what the hell is going on with you and this young-looking old Chink with the gun on me. Oh, and your brother says hi, Wun Thik Dik. He told me to watch out for you."

Wun glared at Rico Morgan and said through clenched teeth, "My brother is a fool, and so are you! You and he will never live to take advantage of our formula, as Wing has. He's living proof that it works and we are about to give it to Sir Phillip and to a few other older, and eminently deserving, members of the British parliament. Too bad you won't see Senator Likkaman turn into a young man. As if you didn't know all this already."

"Actually I didn't. So Wing here is eating babies to keep himself young? How's that work?"

Wing, keeping himself slightly distant from Rico and Zak, stiffened slightly but kept the gun on them. "Mr. Morgan, in case you really didn't figure all this out before now, you should know I am seventy-three years old. I have the physical body of a thirty-year old thanks to a certain mixture created in Germany that features an extraction from the amygdala, parts of the placenta as well as the advanced stem cells of five-month fetuses, and also synthetic sex hormones. There are, of course, other ingredients that will be kept hidden from just about everyone, myself included, but the result creates an enzyme called telomerase, which can reverse aging. My native Chinese scientists did the ground work and tested it somewhat on animals, but only in Germany did the scientists take the final dare and try it on a human. That human was I. I did not go blindly into this. I saw the results in China on mice and monkeys, and offered to be the first human test, but my countrymen refused. They were not yet finished with the testing to the extent they wanted. They did not know the long-term effects. I didn't care. I was about to die from several conjunctive diseases, so it was no risk to me. I gave up on them and traveled to Germany where my fellow Chinese worked in tandem with the scientists there, and was able to obtain enough of the liquid so that I could perform a test on myself. Once it proved efficient, I convinced Dr. Gravenutz to continue giving me the serum. The effect of the mixture is to halt the shortening of the telomere portion of my chromosomes throughout my body, and in fact encourage its regrowth, which has the effect of reversing aging. Surely you must have suspected this from your visit to Germany, to our good doctor Gravenutz. We all thought he had, as you say, spilled the beans."

Sir Phillip took up the tale. "It's a pity Gerta was not able to eliminate you when you were in Germany. That would have saved us immense costs in money and time. You have no idea how much of a pain in the backside you have been to our operation."

Rico looked at Beagle in amazement. "You were behind Gerta's trying to whack me? Why? Did you think I knew all this? I just heard about telomere shortening yesterday. And you say it's a fact? Likkaman is involved? And members of your parliament? I suppose that includes Sir Ovaren Dunwidth? What about Grafter in the U.S.? Are all these guys in on this? Do they all want to look young like Wing here?"

Sir Phillip continued. "I was not behind Gerta. She was hired by your Senator Likkaman, who also arranged for your invitation to Germany. Likkaman informed me of all this after Gerta failed. Mr. Morgan, your pretended ignorance is shameful. We are quite sure you knew all this at least since the incident with Likkaman's nephew LeProsy, certainly since your return from Germany, and some of us even suspected you got the information out of the Arab you killed in the desert in New Mexico."

BORDER CAPER

Sally gave a start and looked at Rico.

Outside on the tarmac the sun was gone and it was now pitch dark. The airport lights glowed dimly here and there, and all was at the moment completely still.

"Of course Likkaman and Grafter are involved," said Wun Thik Dik. They are old men, as are Sir Dunwidth, Sir Grunch, your Henry Pissinjer, and even my compatriot Wu Long Wun." He went on to name six or seven MP's in England, and a few more senators in Washington, DC. "Each of them bought into the New Blue Antiquities club by sending a million dollars in U.S. currency to Chemische Vielfalt in Germany. They are all in line to benefit hugely from the life-giving research done by the Germans and the Chinese."

"So, who ordered the deaths of the border-crossing Mexican girls?" Rico asked. "My guess it was Likkaman, but I also suspect someone in CIA was involved, because one of their agents was nearly killed on a CIA assignment."

Wun Thik Dik responded to Rico's question. "Likkaman was indeed the central factor in the U.S., and he was the one who arranged with his friend Grafter the source of the older stem cells. They had to find a source that no one would bother with, and the border crossings seemed ideal. Many Mexican and South American women with babies at the right stage of development were making their way across the border."

Sir Phillip took up the sordid tale. "We needed the babies to be anywhere from four to six months along, so we had Likkaman use one of his CIA men to contact some members of MS-13 in Mexico to be sure to question the girls about the age of their babies. Once we had some coming with roughly five-month babies we had the Mexican border men alert our Arab team. As you know, they replaced the normal border-crossing man with themselves, and when the girls came along they were operated on. The goods were then shipped to Poughkeepsie to Wun here, or one of his friends, for processing, and the extractions were then air-shipped frozen to Germany. There the extractions were processed, refined, added to, and eventually became the serum. The only problem was, how to dispose of the dead women."

"We heard of one or two found near Chicago. How'd you manage that?"

Sir Phillip continued. "The extraction was done to several women who had already crossed with babies that were not quite at the proper stage of development. We kept track of them and had our team follow them up. In the few months needed for their unborn babies to reach the proper age, these Mexican women were never really accepted into any society, certainly not in the Chicago area, so no fuss was made about their going missing. Chicago was actually better for this, erm, operation than any of the border states because the big lake was handy for disposal services."

"And you were going to expand this operation? Did you think you'd get away with it? It would have meant a lot of dead bodies."

"You see our problem clearly, Mr. Morgan." Sir Phillip smiled.

"So it was Likkaman set up the killing, a guy in CIA contacted the Mexican gangs to get them to play along, and you sit here and wait for the development of the serum. That about right?"

"Mr. Morgan, you now have a clear picture of our operation. I find it hard to believe you did not know all this already."

"Wow,' said Rico. "You guys might end up looking young, but you really need to take something that'd be good for your brains. I can't believe how stupid you all are. Mr. Wun, I was incredibly stupid myself, a while back. I really did think you were concerned with where to put those clever Mexican-made portable toilets for the incoming Mexican workers on that Montana road job, but Sally here pried open my eyes a while back. Not only did I not know all this that you just spelled out, now Sally and Zak here know it too, so obviously, Beagle, your plan was never to let her go. Where were you going to put *our* potties, morons? Bury us here at the airport? Whatta ya think, Mole, do we have enough? I know the audio'll be great, but I sure hope I didn't get in the way of your camera too often."

At the slightly ajar big door leading to the airport tarmac the clear, deep voice of Modesto Pincata Buena said in his best Mexican accent, "*Sí, Señor* Rico. I theenk we got the goods on these sumbitches." He stood there nearly invisible against the now-black sky outside, but the lights in the room clearly showed up the gun in his hand.

Sally gave a gasp and then started to chuckle. Sir Phillip looked around the room as the reality slowly hit him. Wing didn't get it at all until Rico's fist connected with his jaw at the same time his gun hand was slapped out of the way. Wun Thik Dik was not pointing his gun at anyone in particular, and had lowered his gun arm. As Wun brought the gun up to point at the Mexican man in the doorway it flew out of his hand up toward the ceiling as Sally delivered a swift kick to his forearm. The kick was maybe unnecessary because Mole's two double-tapped bullets caught the Chinese man in the chest just as he raised the gun.

Sir Phillip gave a sudden leap toward Sally in the midst of all the chaos, and grabbed her by the arm and put a gun to her head. "Stop!" he cried. "One more move and I'll kill her!"

Sally was about to take some risky action to remove the threat of the gun, but she realized Beagle was too desperate and too dangerous, and she or someone else might get hurt. She looked at Zak, who had been motionless and quiet for most of the action. Zak nodded his head slightly.

Beagle pulled Sally toward the big door. "We're leaving! Anyone who comes after us will have Sally's death on their hands. You, there!" He spoke to Mole. "Come in here and don't try anything."

Mole came in the room but kept his gun on the aging man holding Sally.

Sir Phillip took Sally out of the room by the door, onto the tarmac, out past the large four-wheeled box that was parked next to the wall.

Inside the room Rico and his friend Mole kept the unconscious Wing and the dead Wun silent company, unable to do anything as Sally and Sir Phillip disappeared into the night.

Rico started to say, "I think we should...."

In a commanding tone, Zak Dragon interrupted. "I've got this, Morgan."

Zak pulled a sort of car-door signal device out of his pocket, pushed a button on it, rushed to the big door where Beagle and Sally had passed into the night, and gave a piercing two-tone whistle through the open door. He pointed out onto the tarmac at Sir Phillip, now nearly invisible in the darkness as he walked rapidly away with Sally.

Rico looked at Mole with a question. Mole returned the glance the same way.

In a few seconds they heard a grating, rasping sound like a buzz saw being shoved into a hardwood knot. There was a shout, another louder shout, and then a scream that quickly became a gurgle and rapidly died away to near silence.

There came a sound like the worrying of a dog shaking a rat.

Then all was silence.

Zak said, "Gentlemen, please put your guns away before Backup gets here. He doesn't like them."

Mole found some rope and secured the still unconscious Wing.

Zak slid the big door wider on its rollers and then Rico and Mole could see Sally walking back to the building with a sleek black animal by her side. Beyond them lay a dark, oozing lump on the tarmac. Rico thought the animal with Sally was a dog at first, but then he saw Backup for what he was.

Rico said, "Jeezus Christ, Zak! Sort of like a dog??!!"

CHAPTER 18
Wrap-Up

Two weeks after the events at Heathrow Rico, Modesto, Sally, and Roxy gathered in Rico's Idaho home in his comfortable great room. The only light in the room was provided by a blazing fire in the huge rock fireplace, thirty feet long, which also served to drive away the early Spring chill. Rico invited Zak Dragon but Zak was unable to make the little party. He was busy working with a new young wolf for his guard-animal business. The lively music of Grimes' *Art Angels* CD filled in the background and gave a sparkle to Rico's old house. The two house cats disappeared under the bed when the people started arriving, but Rico's dog Birdie happily greeted all the folks with a smile and a wagging tail.

Mole asked over his beer, "Where's the Control group guys, Rico?"

"They chose to remain incognito, and Kikkie hinted they're already working on another job for us. Prunzy wanted to come but his dad called with some health problem and Prunzy went to visit him at Yale."

"Another job! Come on, Rico!" Sally feigned anger. "Don't you get any time off? Didn't you make enough from this little gig to spend a few days in the sun? It's looking like good Spring weather here in a week or so."

"We got crap weather in DC," said Roxy. Can I stay out here with you a while, Rico?"

Rico blushed, vividly remembering their time together in New Mexico, and said, "Only if Sally says so, and I wouldn't count on it."

Sally noticed the blush but didn't push it. "Rico, you can keep her. I'm going to practice my violin, sadly without that gorgeous leopard purring at me and loving the sound, and take it easy a while. In fact, if Zak lets me, I'll bring Backup over here and sic him on you two! That'll get your backs up!"

Sally continued. "Ya know, one of the oddest things about this whole affair is that Beagle actually pointed Wing out to me after my London concert, yet they were in it together all along. I guess the fact that Wing was there was key. Why not tell me about him, because I'd find out about him soon anyway. And of course Beagle's introducing us acted as a blinder to me about him for quite a while. How could I suspect he was guilty if he'd done that? Fat lot of good it did him. No blue goo could bring him back from what Backup did to him."

"God! I wish I'd been there to see that," said Roxy. The leopard just offed that Beagle guy?"

"Yes indeed," replied Mole. "It wasn't pretty. Backup chewed the living shit out of Beagle's neck. Hell, his head was nearly off. He was thoroughly dead long before we got to him. Zak put ol' Backup-baby into his box and we went to see Beagle, but we couldn't do anything for him. Zak made a phone call — I dunno to who — and the next day the newspapers had it that Sir Phillip Beagle had an unhappy encounter with the propeller of a private airplane while wandering about the airport in the dark. The paper also had it that Sir Ovaren Dunwidth left the country on urgent government business. Zak's contacts told him, and he told us, Dunwidth is in fact in a British slammer, never more to be seen, along with three other less-prominent MP's that Dunwidth ratted out. What a bunch of bastards, eh?"

Yessir," replied Roxy. She drained her beer, went to the kitchen for two more and handed one to Mole.

"Senator Likkaman is also in jail, along with Grafter and a few other good ol' boys." Rico took a hit on his Scotch and soda. "One thing came up that interests me. It's a recording of Likkaman and Grafter with Wun Thik Dik talking about hiring another goon to whack Mexican girls. They pretty much committed themselves to jail with that, which is why Congress and the President and the grand jury didn't lose any time convicting them of murder. But where in hell did that recording come from? You know anything about that, Roxy?"

"No. It didn't come from our group, so far as I know. Only that one CIA fellow that Likkaman contacted to send me to New Mex, Clipps, I think his name was..."

Rico cut in. "Yes, Richard Clipps."

"Only Dick Clipps in CIA was involved with Likkaman, so far as we've found out. But no recording, no."

Mole spoke. "Looks like someone else was onto them. Someone able to put a tap on 'em, and knew enough to look at the right guys. That's suspiciously interesting."

"Yes," said Rico, "but the best thing is it helped nail 'em good."

"It's a mystery indeed," said Sally. To herself she said, "And thank you very much, Gwen Fairbanks, NSA recording specialist." She asked the group, "Whatever happened to the

German girl who tried to whack you, Rico? And what about that German scientist?"

Rico took another hit on his drink. "Doctor Gravenutz is off scot-free. He didn't break any laws. All he did was supply Wing Hung Lo with that blue goo. They couldn't tie the good doctor into receiving baby parts. The stuff arrived in Germany as a frozen extract, so he couldn't be tagged with any viable link to crime. I know he was in contact with Likkaman, though, because Gravenutz knew I was from Idaho without my telling him. And Likkaman set up the hit on me over there, which was the only reason I was invited to Germany in the first place.

"The German girl Gerta is still at large, and Mole, we may yet have to deal with her some fine day. Boise Control found out through the German military guys she had some connection with Achmed and the other Mideasterner, but no one knows whose payroll she's on. Likkaman may have hired her for the hit on me, but he was probably just tapping an available asset funded by who knows who. She could be based in Germany or maybe China, or England or even the U.S. We know Beagle helped put her onto me when I went to Germany with info fed to him by Likkaman.

"The Chinese girl Wun Fan Phuk was supposed to pick me up, per the arrangements Boise Control made with the test facility. Part of that too was bogus. The invite of course came via the bad guys, and when Boise Control contacted the test facility to confirm the invitation was genuine, the German company seemed to think I was just an incoming journalist, or someone similar, to have a quick look around. Together with Willie Kers, who knew her brother, they got Wun Fan Phuk to pick me up. But Gerta got to me first. The easiest way to intercept me would have been for Gravenutz to send Gerta, rather than Fan Phuk. Gravenutz denied this of course, and it's believable because he should also have been able to stop Fan Phuk from coming. But Fan Phuk did come. She saw that Gerta was there ahead of her and followed along, thereby saving my sorry ass."

Mole added, "Gerta may be connected to the old bitch who's the head German politico. She'd eat babies for breakfast if it'd let her stay young. Gerta may have been hired by her, and could be Teutonic or even Islamic. No one knows."

Roxy frowned and said, "We at CIA suspected Abe in Japan, Xi in China, Trudeau in Canada and Merkel in Germany of knowing about this Chinese-German operation to halt aging, and of course we suspected each and all of the elder politicians, past and present, in this country, but they've all managed to keep out of the limelight. So have all the really wealthy old men and women, for that matter."

"Or they may know nothing about it at all, being honest enough to age gracefully." Mole sipped his beer.

"Crap! I doubt that!" Rico emptied his glass.

Mole asked, "What was Wing doing in England? Showing off?"

Sally answered, "I suspect he was doing just that, giving the geezers a look at what their support and their money could do for them if they only had enough of it, and more dead babies. But that's just a guess."

"I think it's a mighty good guess, darlin'," said Rico. "The old farts needed proof the stuff worked, and his visit there might have been a push for more money as well.

"¡*Claro*!" Mole said. "The bastard sure did look young."

"Well," said Rico, "we made out all right financially. I got a small token from a certain friend in Washington, DC, above and beyond the reimbursement from Immigration. My friend was pleased we managed to clean up this sordid affair and keep it all out of the funny papers. I'll share it with y'all."

Mole smiled. "Why don't you just say it was from the President, *amigo*? We all know he's almost a buddy of yours, and he's great at making deals, eh? What better deal than to pay you to clean up some of the dismal swamp dwellers in DC, Likadik and Grafter and at least three more of those bastards."

"Four more, actually," replied Rico, "and that turd Clipps from CIA who worked with MS-13 makes five. And let's not forget the dear departed Wing Hung Lo. It didn't take long for him to get his reward once he was stuck in a jail cell."

"I'm not sure I understand why he croaked so fast." Mole spoke with a frown. "I guess it's because of his not having access to the blue goo any more. But if he was looking that young, how could he have reverted to what amounts to old age so fast? The report said he died with what amounted to heart failure with complications associated with old age. Basically he ran out of gas, but that doesn't really make a lot of sense."

"I heard a pretty good explanation from Yeats's dad," said Rico, referring to Sukkan Dondem Prunzalot, father of the headman at Boise Control. "He said Wing was not really growing younger. His injections gave him a false sort of double-telomere effect in his DNA. I don't begin to understand it and told him so, so he asked Yeats to give me an analogy. 'Imagine a balloon with a slow leak,' Yeats said. 'As long as you pump air into the balloon it stays round and full, and can even grow larger if you pump enough air into it. But as soon as you stop with the air, or in Wing's case the daily injections, the balloon quickly deflates to nothing. And that is why Mr. Wing is no longer with us.' That made some sense to me."

Sally replied, "So all this death, these murdered girls, was for nothing? The blue stuff was just a mask, not a cure?"

"Not necessarily." Roxy took up the discussion. "Of course it was tragic, but ongoing tests in China and Germany might, someday, come up with something that will actually retard aging. The Russians too are doing similar research. But whatever the scientists come up with has to be done without the use of five-month-old babies. What I mean is, the deaths of these women might actually help save lives in the distant future."

Mole broke in. "I can't call it a good piece of scientific advancement, no matter what good might come of it. There ought to have been a better way, a legal and moral way to find out what gives inside our deep, dark DNA."

Sally agreed. "Roxy, I'm not sure I can call anything about this deal good no matter what comes of it. The Chinese and German scientists haven't been shut down. All that's stopped is their use of dead babies, *that we know about*. What'll they try next? Raiding war zones for just-dead heroes? Cyborgs? Hybrids? Other types of ghouls? Yuk!"

"Speaking of ghouls," Rico said, "a certain, er, acquaintance in Mexico sent me ten boxes of Cuban stogies as a way of saying thank you for getting to the bottom of this. One of the boxes of Cohibas marked "Open First" had a big check inside, right inside the box, sealed up in Havana. That man has long tentacles. Actually I feel somewhat sorry for the poor bastard. He doesn't get to have his love child, and nothing can make that up to him. He really had strong feelings for that dead girl. He had her portrait done in oil and it was hanging in his study."

Sally smiled. "Rico, I'm gonna write that down. You're feeling sorry for a Mexican drug lord."

Roxy replied. "If I were in his place I'd feel pretty lousy too, even though I might have taken some revenge on one of the perpetrators. Nothing can make up for losing a child."

Mole added, "No revenge can bring back someone you've lost. That's not an easy thing to get over, drug lord or not."

The happy gathering took on a slightly somber mood. The upbeat Grimes album had quit, and silence filled the room. The low light from the fireplace grew gradually dimmer as the once-flaming logs turned to embers. The four friends sat together in peaceful silence.

BORDER CAPER

CREATED BY SHEEP CREEK PUBLISHING, NORTH FORK, ID 83466

RAY ORDORICA